Kaitlyn Wolfe – Crown Attorney
Expanded version

Jacqui Morrison

Lachesis
Publishing
www.lachesispublishing.com

Published Internationally by Lachesis Publishing
1787 Cartier Court, RR 1,
Kingston, Nova Scotia, B0P 1R0

National Library of Canada Cataloguing in Publication
Data

A catalogue record for this book is available from the
National Library of Canada.

ISBN 1-897370-14-8
Also available in multiple eBook formats from
www.lachesispublishing.com
ISBN 1-897370-15-6

This is a work of fiction. Names, characters, places and
incidents are either the product of the author's
imagination or are used fictitiously, and any resemblance
to any person or persons, living or dead, events, or
locales is entirely coincidental.

Review

Kaitlyn Wolfe is a tale of determination and self-empowerment, a must-read for those concerned with both women's and native issues.

—Steven Duff, author of *Raiders of the Lost Barque, Land of the People Apart, The Wanderer's Storm-Song, Hunter of Dreams* and *The Osterling Weekend*

.

Teaser

Holly Nelson cowered in what her lover, Frank Jordan, called his panic place – a false space behind one wall of the bedroom of Frank's condo, approximately two feet deep.

"… check the place for his bitch … waste her too …" she heard through the plaster wall. Surrounded by countless kilos of marijuana, she clenched her teeth against a squeal that would surely give her away.

Two men, having hurdled the building's electronic entry code, busted in on Frank slumped into his recliner listening to dance club music on his surround sound stereo.

Caught unaware, Frank had been unable to reach the panic room, but during the scuffle outside the bedroom, Holly dove for cover and secured the door from the inside. Now she was in darkness, straining to listen.

The stereo was abruptly turned up. She swallowed hard, her body stiffened, and she dared not breathe. Suddenly, two sharp thuds broke through the music. Her body began to tremble.

She looked down at her shaking hands and willed them to still, but they wouldn't stop. Her body refused to obey her command.

Footsteps became clearer. The men had entered the bedroom.

She recognized the sound of sliding doors. The men were now rooting in the closet. The clink of clothes hangers and the rustle of clothing being chucked about confirmed her assumption.

Earlier, a business associate of Frank's, a man he addressed as Marty, had shown up unannounced for a none-too-friendly conversation about how Frank's lifestyle was drawing attention to 'the operation'.

Frank had been rattled by the drop in and when Marty left, he blurted out for her to get ready, defying the warning. They would go out on the town.

She had been getting ready, and not happily at that

when the goons had entered the condo.

Frank had built the panic place himself and hidden the entrance behind a pivoting chest of drawers. A chest of drawers now a hair's breath away from the men seeking Holly out.

A phone rang. Holly startled and slipped to the floor then gasped quietly. She froze. The phone in the bedroom rang again. Holly stopped breathing. A frightening pause followed.

"You want me to pick that up, Wally? See if it's her?"

"Are you insane?"

"Sorry, Wally, I wasn't thinking." A silence filled the bedroom.

Had they spotted the panic room door? She went stiff as a board.

"She's not here, Wally."

She breathed a silent sigh of relief.

"Shit! Well, she'll turn up somewhere. And when she does …. Let's go."

Yes. Yes. Holly willed them out – out of the apartment.

The sound of their footsteps waned and a door shut, barely audible.

Just in case their leaving was a ruse to bring her out of her hiding place, Holly watched the glowing minute hand on her Rolex indicating time passing. She remained trapped in her refuge for ten, long additional minutes.

What would she find when she came out, Frank's lifeless body? She hoped they hadn't blown his brains out. What a mess that would be to clean up.

What was she thinking? She couldn't stay in the apartment with a dead man!

She'd gather a spare change of clothes then flee and never return to this dump.

What if they had someone watching the building entrance? She gave herself a mental shake.

One thing she knew. She couldn't stay here.

Dedication

Kaitlyn Wolfe, Crown Attorney, new and expanded version is dedicated to my father, the late Dr. John Sinclair Morrison. Dad was my inspiration, my editor (from the time I learned how to read) and a friend to all.

Grateful recognition is given to Sandy Aldworth, Brenda Gies-Switzer, Steven Duff, Shannon Mills, Fran Whittaker, Lucy Ethier-Fournier and Lenore Hawley.

Sincere appreciation goes to George Green who granted use of the photograph for the front cover. The photograph was the inspiration for Kaitlyn's mystical cave.

Thank you to Wayne and Alison Daub for always being there. *Miigwetch!*

Kaitlyn Wolfe – Crown Attorney

Chapter One

Susan Waberay spied the bedroom entrance, then, in a conspiring tone, asked Kaitlyn Wolfe, "Can you sneak out of the house Saturday night?"

After a two-week hiatus, the two teenage girlfriends had re-connected, and that afternoon on a dreary Wednesday, Kaitlyn's friend had come over for a joint homework session.

Having never felt the urge to sneak around her mother, Kaitlyn was utterly puzzled. "Sneak out? What the devil for?"

Susan leaned toward her, mischief written plain on her face. "Brad Collins, the captain of the football team, is having a party at his parents' house," she breathed and declared, "... and we're going."

"Why don't I just ask?"

Rolling her eyes, the teen's universal expression of 'duuh?' Susan explained with strained patience, "Brad's parents will be away for the weekend. There will be no one to chaperone the party. Knowing your mom, she'd call Mrs. Collins. And that will screw it up for all of us."

"I could tell her I'm going to a movie with you and then sleeping over at your place." But Kaitlyn was uncomfortable; the lie was eating up at her insides already.

A victory smile spread on her friend's face. "That'll work! She'll never check with Ida and Ida won't care if we come back late."

Having never heard anyone her age call a parent anything but mom or dad, Kaitlyn felt Susan was being disrespectful. "Why do you call your mom Ida?"

"If she was a real mom, she'd handle her problems instead of making me cover up for her. If she can't respect herself, then why should I respect her?"

"You have a point," Kaitlyn said with reluctance while shaking her head sadly. "Margaret is a great mom." Uttering her mother's name for the first time felt so grown up.

* * * *

Saturday quickly rolled in, and carrying a change of clothing in a duffel bag, Kaitlyn arrived at Susan's house. They both rushed to her friend's bedroom, and changed.

Sue ditched her jeans to slip on a form-fitting, mid-thigh length skirt with a tight shirt that accentuated her burgeoning figure.

"You look hot, Sue!"

Her friend grinned broadly at the compliment then grimaced, sighing aloud at the sight of her overalls. "You don't. Wait there." Sue went rooting in her closet. She pulled out another of her skirts and chucked it at her. "You will too with this."

Kaitlyn pulled on the offered skirt and her tight T-shirt. She caught her reflection in Susan's mirror. She'd never dared to wear a mini-skirt before.

My tanned legs look really long. Mom would kill me if she saw how skimpily I'm dressed. But for this time, one time ....

Even with prodding, Kaitlyn refused to smear on make-up while Susan's chocolate brown eyes shimmered with aqua eyeshadow and her lips glistened the color of a red fire engine.

Both heard the honking of a truck.

"That would be our ride, my cousin Vern," Susan said, reaching for her purse.

They slipped outside and into the front seat of the truck. As if to impress them, Vern peeled off from the rocky driveway. Once he had merged unto a two-way lane, he cleared his throat and spoke in his new, deep man's voice, "Don't forget for a moment that some of these guys are pigs who only want to get into your pants. I'll watch out for you, but don't go into any of the bedrooms for any reason, you hear? If you like a guy, give him your phone number and meet up with him another time. Under no circumstances do I want either of you making out with any of the football players."

Susan whipped around to Vern. "How pompous can you get? Under no circumstances ...." She gave him a shove. With a tone that mimicked his previous authority, she reminded him, "You're my cousin, not my mother. I can handle things myself."

Vern took the shove with good humour but sobered. "Oh, yeah. And another thing, don't leave a drink unattended. Have you heard of acid?"

Kaitlyn's stomach went into a knot. Had she made a foolish decision in agreeing to put herself at risk? "Oh, my God, are you serious? Could they ... burn our tongues!"

Vern spared her a quick glance. "Kaitlyn, for such a smart girl, you're really a goof. Acid is a street name for L.S.D. The drug makes you hallucinate. If it is slipped into your drink, you would totally lose your inhibitions. Only God knows what you'd do then."

Kaitlyn relaxed and the drive continued in agreeable silence until Vern turned the vehicle onto a side road. "One girl from River Deer Territory took some LSD, then she made it with three guys." He shrugged, laughing a little. "She was kind of a skank to begin with. Now she's fifteen, knocked up, and labeled a slut on her reserve."

"Enough, Vern," Susan warned, adding, "That's so gross!"

Vern pulled into an empty spot near the party house, turned the ignition off, and turned to both girls. "Not only gross, but she pretty well wrecked her life."

Avoiding Susan's friendly slap, Vern went on. "Just dance, have fun, and I'll watch your back. Don't do anything with any guys, or you'll get a reputation just like that girl." He gave them a curt nod, and as if it were agreed upon, he opened the driver side door and slipped out.

Susan scooted over to Vern's recently vacated seat and reached out a hand. "We hear you, brother protector! Now help me out." Vern assisted Susan out of the truck and gave her a big, wet raspberry. Kaitlyn followed suit in exiting the vehicle.

Vern knocked on Brad's front door and entered. Susan went in next, and Kaitlyn closed the door behind her.

Kaitlyn scanned the crowd within. Well over twenty-five kids, ranging from fourteen to eighteen, were already in a partying mood and mingling. Wisely, Brad had removed the breakables, the cluttering furniture from the living room, and covered his mom's sofa with a blanket. Her gaze fell on three massive guys in football jerseys. They took turns in pouring beer from a keg into plastic glasses.

Vern quickly rounded up three glasses for their small group. As he handed one to each of them, he gave them a reminder. "Remember what I said." He nodded curtly then left them on their own.

Kaitlyn raised her glass, peered through the golden liquid, and sniffed at its head of foam. She shrugged and ventured a sip of the beer for the very first time.

"Yuck! It tastes disgusting," she gasped, unable to mask her disgust. She watched in amazement as Susan took a deep swig, then chocked some after she swallowed it.

"Eww! You've got that right!" Susan was still trying to shake off the awful taste. "Let's control our disgust," Susan added, "so we don't look like losers. Let's just pry sips down our throat. When it's done, we'll dance."

They nursed their beers, watching the dancing moves of the others on the makeshift dance floor until

Kaitlyn's spirits fell. She'd spotted Stacey Cummings and her best friend, Gwen Gleeson, coming through the front door.

Stacey, her nemesis, was clutching Mike Smith's arm. Even from afar, her eyes seemed glazed over. Kaitlyn's first thought was that she was likely already drunk. Gwen, Stacey's puppy, strolled in solo behind the couple. She was dressed to pick up guys.

Mike ditched his date and her friend nearby to fetch drinks. Stacey panned the room, and her glance fell on Kaitlyn.

She elbowed Gwen, a disgusted look evident on her face, and let out for everyone within earshot to hear, "God, those scuzzy welfare people are here. Can't get away from them."

Determined to ignore the bullies, Kaitlyn held her head high.

Lowering her voice to what she thought was a whisper, Stacey conspired, "I will make it so they never come to one of Brad's parties again," she added in a whining tone, "it's only supposed to be the popular people here."

"Stacey," Gwen pled, moving to block Stacey's view of Susan and herself. "The party is big enough. We can just ignore them. Don't stir it up, have fun with Mike. Just leave them be."

Hatred filled Stacey's facial expression. "No way, they need to learn a lesson, learn their place."

Kaitlyn mentally shook her head. She had expected such an answer, having been the victim of Stacey's streak of meanness and stubbornness since the first grade. And Stacey nurtured her qualities on a daily basis.

Visibly shaking her head and raising a hand in defeat, Gwen relented, distancing herself. "Whatever. Sometimes you can be so cruel. Leave them be." But hearing Gwen's words did not soothe Kaitlyn's mood.

Stacey verbally attacked Gwen's retreating form. "You were nothing before I let you hang with me."

Knowing how Stacey operated, Kaitlyn cringed at the drilling Gwen was about to get.

"You'd better shut up, Gwen, or you'll spend the next four years at the library instead of at parties with me." Poor Gwen looked as if she had been slapped.

She froze then returned to her friend's side. "I'm sorry, Stacey. It must be the beer talking. I just want you to have a good time with Mike and not worry about scummy people."

Kaitlyn couldn't believe the sight before her. Gwen was desperate, sucking up to Stacey.

Stacey gave Gwen a long stare as if reconsidering her threat. "Apology accepted," she said loftily.

Kaitlyn was so saddened to see how much control this bully exercised over even her own best friend. She sighed heavily, letting the matter go.

Susan and her finished their bitter beer and coaxed each other to join a fast dance they liked. *Stayin' Alive* by the popular Australian band the Bee Gees had everyone in the middle of the room doing their best moves.

Nobody else seems to mind their Native status. Kaitlyn filled her lungs with a soothing breath. Evidently, there were still young people who had not yet been trained in the fine art of discrimination.

Vern left his football friends and joined them on the dance floor. "I'm parched," Susan claimed between dances – Vern's cue to get them two more beers.

Despite feeling a bit light-headed from the first one, Kaitlyn accepted the second beer. She would have much preferred a Mountain Dew, but a previous glance to the table where drinks were lined up for the taking confirmed no soft drinks were being served. Maybe Mountain Dew was for dweebs.

She was sipping, forcing the vile stuff between her lips when Brad, the host, grabbed her arm. "Come on, let's dance!" He coaxed her until she relented.

Pleased at being asked by the greatest catch of the football team, Kaitlyn put her beer glass on the nearest table, and with elation, she followed Brad into the dancing crowd. After the second fast dance, Brad thanked her politely and then took a turn on the floor with Susan.

Her mood fell. Brad was just being nice to all his guests. That was fine with her; she could appreciate a touch of class when she saw it. She sipped more beer, distancing each sip but still trying to re-hydrate herself without any head-rushes.

Despite Stacey's presence and nasty disposition, Kaitlyn was enjoying herself. Until her head began spinning. She plunked herself in the first available seat, in the nick of time as she was about to fall flat on the floor.

To her dismay, even seated on the sofa, the room kept on spinning. Had she drank the beer too quickly? Remembering the bitter taste, she quickly dismissed the notion.

Mere seconds passed and she felt the color draining from her face. She'd never felt this horrible before now. Panic usurped her earlier fun feelings. Something was terribly wrong.

Susan must have noticed her state because Kaitlyn became aware of her presence when she dropped to her knees before her. "Kaitlyn, what's the matter? You look like crap."

"I'm sick, real sick. Get Vern. Oh, God ...." Kaitlyn closed her eyes and grimaced against a bout of nausea.

Susan patted her knee, reassuring her. "I'll get Vern."

Susan returned with Vern who took charge immediately, carrying her out to the truck. Despite the fact that Kaitlyn had ordered Vern to take her home, he sped away in the opposite direction from her house. Right to the emergency department, he'd told her.

* * * *

Vern gently placed her onto the first available gurney in

the hallway. She was so grateful for his care.

Kaitlyn caught sight of the duty doctor bent over a file at the nurses' station. He raised his glance and looked them over with disdain.

"What kind of drug is this girl on?" he called to Vern in a contemptuous manner over the whimpers of other patients. Kaitlyn shook her head to convey that she hadn't taken drugs, but her poor state got the better of her and she gave up in her protest, lying prone on the gurney.

"Nothing," blustered Vern who visibly swallowed hard as the doctor neared. "We were out at a party and she just started to get dizzy, feeling sickly." Vern stepped aside.

The doctor pulled out a penlight from his shirt pocket and shined a light in her eyes. "She's on something."

Vern shook his head vehemently. "She's had two beers. She doesn't do drugs."

The doctor's declaration horrified Kaitlyn. "How could that be?" she mumbled weakly.

The doctor motioned for a nurse to assist. As she neared the group, he explained to her. "I'll have to pump her stomach." He whipped around to Vern. "Where are her parents?"

Vern looked to Susan for guidance but she remained silent. "At home," Vern provided with hesitation.

"Get them on the phone," the doctor snapped at Vern, as if the entire situation were his fault. "I need their permission to pump her stomach in order to save her life."

Back in a foetal position, Kaitlyn watched Vern hurry to the nurse's station. After a short exchange on the phone, he called the Doctor over and passed him the earpiece. The doctor was likely explaining her situation. The doctor's nod told Kaitlyn that he'd gotten permission.

She was quickly wheeled into a treatment room, and without any delay, the doctor started the procedure.

Less than thirty minutes later, voices in the hallway revealed that her mom with younger brother Nathan had arrived at the emergency department.

* * * *

With a sullen-face, Vern greeted Margaret along with a petrified Susan. Next to pull through the emergency doors were two police officers. Panic filled his chest.

Constable Crewman rounded Margaret to reach the E.R. counter. He gave her a curt nod adding, "Hello, Mrs. Wolfe." Then all business he turned to the nurse in charge.

Margaret smiled briefly at the officers who had been co-workers and good friends of her late husband.

To Vern, it was evident from the head nurse's address to his Aunt Margaret and the constable that she knew them both. She motioned the constable to a private area and asked Margaret to take a seat.

Despite their low voices, Vern overhead their conversation. The nurse explained how Kaitlyn had perhaps attempted suicide. Vern became livid. The head nurse was also adding her personal suspicion that the cause might have been due to her recent loss of her father.

Vern's outrage waned when his aunt bee-lined toward him. She grabbed at his arm. "What the hell is going on, Vern?" She eyed him with suspicion. "Kaitlyn went to a movie. How can she need to have her stomach pumped?"

"Aunt Margaret, I think Kaitlyn parked a ... soda on a table, left it unattended. A kid might have put some drug in her drink as a joke. I don't think it was meant to hurt her, Aunt Margaret."

His aunt glared at both of them in turn. Suspicion that the whole story hadn't yet been revealed became glaring by her narrowing stare.

"Just where were you tonight? And don't give me any more nonsense about soda! The doctor smelled beer on her breath."

With a guilty demeanor, Susan explained about the unchaperoned party. They had gone only to have a night of dancing, not to get wasted, she'd insisted.

Susan then admitted sharing Vern's theory, having witnessed Kaitlyn putting down her beer to share a couple of dances with Brad, the host.

Outraged, Margaret marched to the nurse, leaving him and Susan standing guiltily in the waiting room. "My daughter's friend thinks someone spiked her beer as a joke."

The nurse looked around Aunt Margaret's frame, her lower jaw hanging wide open. She quickly recovered from her shock adding, "Some joke. I'd better tell the doctor."

Ten minutes later the doctor emerged from the curtained area and went straight to Aunt Margaret. "Mrs. Wolfe?" She rose, nodding. "We administered activated charcoal to your daughter to purge the drugs out of her system before much more of it found its way into her bloodstream. She should begin throwing up at any moment."

Already, preliminary moans from behind the curtains reached their group.

"Mrs. Wolfe." The doctor pocketed his hands in his lab coat. "Regulations dictate that the police be notified." Aunt Margaret nodded toward the constables off to the side. "I called them in. They'll take a sample of the discharge. If someone did indeed try to poison your daughter, the discharge becomes evidence to charge the culprit who did this to her."

Constable Crewman approached the group. "Mrs. Wolfe, I had no idea that the case involved your daughter. The dispatch service never said the name of the patient."

"Call me Margaret." She waved her hand in the direction of Susan and him. "Question her friends and track down the creep who did this to my daughter."

* * * *

Margaret's nephew, Vern, and Susan Waberay, sang like birds when questioned. Constable Crewman radioed a second police car and appraised that officer to the situation. He turned to Margaret with compassion in his regard. "Another police team has been dispatched to this Brad Collin's house."

* * * *

From the open doorway to the house where the alleged drugging took place, the staff sergeant witnessed a clumsy teen attempt to hide the beer. "The beer could be the least of your problems, son," he hollered over the chattering guests who now cowered in the farthest corner of the living room. His subordinate officers and he entered the room.

Having garnered their full attention, the staff sergeant ordered, "Listen up." The chatter went dead. Having all eyes on him, he instructed, "This is what's going to happen. First, my officers and I will search all of you. Anyone found with drugs will immediately be arrested." A few brazen teens edged toward the kitchen doorway. The staff sergeant whistled, gaining their attention and stopping their defiance. "Anyone trying to take off will meet the same fate." He motioned them to cluster with the other teens. "Everybody stays in this room. Officers will call your parents to have you picked up. No one leaves the premises without a parent or an adult. If you don't have someone that can pick you up, I'll arrest you for underage drinking. Got it? This way no one can lie and say their parents are away."

"That's not fair!" whined a young man.

The staff sergeant locked gazes with him. "What's your name?"

With reluctance, the senior answered, "Duncan Cross."

"Well then, Duncan, you won the search lottery.

Officer, search that boy."

Constable Fletcher finished patting Duncan down and returned a curt nod. "He's clean, sarge." He then moved to the Cummings girl standing next to the Duncan boy.

She resisted. "Do any of you goons know who my father is? He owns this town."

The staff sergeant shook his head at the misplaced display of power while he neared her. "Ms. Cummings, you just said the wrong thing to the wrong people at the wrong time, just like your lippy friend there. Your father has no jurisdiction, authority, or influence over the Ontario Provincial Police." He gave her a don't-give-me-any-lip look. "You will be treated like any of the other underage drinkers present. Hand over your clutch purse."

The still-fuming girl reluctantly reached out a hand, handing over her purse. He grabbed and opened it. He soon spied a suspicious clear plastic bag and pulled it out. On further inspection, he mentally labeled six tablets as LSD.

He fixed the young lady with a lengthy stare. "You have the right to remain silent—"

Her ill-advised bravado back, the Cummings girl screeched, interrupting her being mirandized. "My dad will have your badge for talking to me like this. Gwen, call my dad now. Right now!"

He sought who the defiant girl was addressing. He gave Gwen a stare that stopped any action she might have intended. "Sorry, Ms. Cummings, but your friend is next in being searched. If she's clean, she may use the phone." He returned to the Miranda warning on the Cummings girl while his partner searched Gwen's belongings.

Young Gwen carried no drugs and she held herself together, appearing sober. He allowed her to use the telephone as a ranting Ms. Cummings was escorted to a police car.

Mike Smith, young Ms. Cummings' date, also

carried illigal drugs in a front jeans pocket. A small bag of marijuana. No LSD was found on his person. He was also arrested and joined his date in the police car. By his bewildered expression, he obviously hadn't envisioned his date with Ms. Cummings ending in this fashion.

* * * *

Kaitlyn awoke during daylight, a lunch tray left forgotten on her hospital table. Her headache was so intense that she wished she would die. Her mouth felt and tasted like a rat sewer.

So this was a hangover.

She recalled hearing school chums boasting about their epic hangovers during recesses, as if it were some sort of contest, but, if this ranked as one of life's great accomplishments, Kaitlyn wanted no part of it.

Feeling the need to tidy herself up, she sought the bathroom. She gazed at a frightful image of herself in the mirror, thinking of the moment when she first woke up in the emergency department. A sensation like coming up from a deep dive overtook her then.

The sound of footsteps had her turn around. Seeing her mom, she rushed to her and embraced her, only too aware of the look of shame on her face.

After they both recovered from a bout of crying, her mom drew her back, shaking her head sadly. "Child, First Nations people have to stay away from alcohol, for the sake of both health and reputation. Your presence at this infamous party embarrassed all the people of Wanitou."

Having heard quite enough already, Kaitlyn rolled her eyes in teenage eloquence.

Her mother wept quietly until she regained her composure. "I just lost your father, and if I lost you, I'd die inside. Kaitlyn, you and Nathan are all that's keeping me alive."

Those words deeply affected Kaitlyn. Feeling the goose bumps on her arms, she knew without a doubt that she would never forget them.

Kaitlyn embraced her mom for what seemed like an eternity. Once she released her mom, she was grounded from seeing her friends after class, for the next two weeks.

What would she do with the two weeks that she would be housebound? That meant no sports, no Susan, and no television. Her Mom meant for her to remember that mistake, forever, and learn from it.

* * * *

After being released from the hospital, they drove home silently. Her mother seemed to drive the station wagon over every bump and pot hole along the dirt road.

Once home, a thorough brushing of teeth and a scalding hot shower improved her hangover and her state of mind. After a plain toast and an apple juice, Kaitlyn got her mom's permission to take a walk in the fresh air to clear her stubborn headache.

She hurried over to Susan's house without phoning ahead, as was her custom, so she could let her friend know of her grounding.

Susan opened the front door and grimaced. "You look like crap." She motioned Kaitlyn inside the house.

"I know." Kaitlyn was all too aware of her tear-stained face. "I had to get out of the house. Mom's so mad at me; I feel so ashamed at having lied to her. Her pleading eyes are killing me. This morning when I entered the kitchen, she looked up at me the way she did after dad died." She swallowed a sob. "I just had to tell you of my grounding."

"I expected you to be grounded."

"For the next two whole weeks. No Friends, no sport, no television." Kaitlyn shook her head at her fate. "I've really messed up. Plus, that might cost me a spot on the cross-country team. I trained so hard for it." Kaitlyn choked up.

Susan patted her shoulder. "It's not your fault. It's

Stacey's." She huffed in hatred. "It has to be her that put the drug into your beer."

Kaitlyn lifted a guilty gaze to Susan. "But Vern warned us not to leave our drinks unattended and, well, I was having so much fun dancing. I screwed up." Kaitlyn felt the weight of her stupidity. "Are you grounded as well?"

"Nope. Remember it's Ida. She yelled at me and then she went off brooding. She's such a loser."

"Don't say that about your mom, Susan. She's not that bad." Feeling minutes were ticking off, Kaitlyn quickly added, "Anyway, I better get back before mom finds out I used the walk to speak to you. She'd ground me for life then."

Susan nodded reassuringly and with a parting, "Yeah, you better." She closed the door.

* * * *

Life went on, and her two-week grounding period expired. Kaitlyn attended her next running practice, fully expecting to be let go from the team. She thought the moment was upon her when Coach Stinson motioned her aside from the group.

"Natural ability is wonderful," Coach Stinson said then she paused while assessing Kaitlyn. "But it is nothing without commitment, focus, and self-discipline." She smiled at Kaitlyn. "You, my dear Kaitlyn, have all of those things, so keep on doing what you're doing." Walking away from the exchange, Kaitlyn breathed a sigh of relief. Someone must have tipped Coach Stinson of her ordeal and subsequent grounding.

Kaitlyn casually told her mom about making the team, as though it were a trivial matter, over supper. Her strategy was she didn't want to draw undue attention to herself following the dreadful incident that caused such pain to her mother.

* * * *

The following Friday, Kaitlyn competed in her first cross-country run. Despite stomach flutters, she came in third in the grade nine category. Coach Stinson assured her that with more practice and seasoning, her potential to win many more meets was all but certain.

The only sad moment of her day came when Connie refused to talk to her. Stacey's older sister and team member, who had been giving Kaitlyn the odd lift home after practice, now averted her eyes every time Kaitlyn got near her. Connie had become a supporter of her spoiled sister and her new behavior spoke of blame as if Kaitlyn were responsible for her young sister's arrest.

Blustery cold days followed and then a warm, golden haze settled over the northern countryside. Indian summer was the popular designation, but in Wanitou, it was commonly referred to Aboriginally-enhanced Climatic Preservation.

Her mom had started a new job, which she loved. Isobel, the supervisor, let her mom work from nine to three Monday to Thursday. Even without the death benefits from the O.P.P., their family could get by on her mom working the four days a week. Kaitlyn assumed her mom wanted to keep her mind busy.

Early, on the second weekend in October, the day was cool but sunny. Her entire family, including her best friend Susan, Leslie and Buck, Susan's siblings, all packed into a borrowed minivan while her mom, a large picnic basket in tow, settled in last. They drove to Sudbury where the regional track meet was hosted. They arrived at the conservation area by nine that morning, well in time for her race scheduled for ten that morning.

Kaitlyn introduced Coach Stinson to her mom. Her coach boasted that she was an asset to the team, which elated her.

She dedicated the next hour to all of the warm-up stretches, a necessity to avoid any muscle injury. It was boring, but a necessary evil, like washing dishes. The preparation was also part of her self-imposed regimen that so impressed her coach, who briefly interrupted her to give her a short word on her main competition and a run-down of the course.

The run consisted of a five kilometer tract that included steep hills, shallow streams, and narrow nature paths.

The call for her age group came quickly to Kailtyn. In a daze, she found herself at the start off line amongst fourteen other athletes from a wide variety of schools throughout northern Ontario. The bang of the starter pistol had her sprinting off the starting gate without a conscious effort on her part. She and her main adversary, a competitor named Rose Carter, took the lead, feet thudding frenetically and breath whooshing rhythmically.

Once her rhythm was established, Kaitlyn glanced at Rose. She was wiry where Kaitlyn was slender and lean.

Rose Carter had arrived in Sudbury back in September from Toronto. A seasoned competitor, she had been in cross-country racing since grade five. She had compiled a formidable reputation for her stamina and solid performance. Per Coach Stinson who made it her business to know the competition, Rose was particularly adept at handling hills.

Kaitlyn kept up neck and neck for the first mile. A hill loomed and she gathered her inner strength, forcing herself to take the lead up the hill, a move to deter the competition mentally, but Rose also put on extra effort, tail-gating her so closely that she expected to be overtaken at any moment. Kaitlyn now silently agreed with Coach Stinson's assumption; Rose's experience showed.

The top of hill led the way to a nature trail which ran through scraggly brush in much need of trimming. Kaitlyn ducked and weaved so as to avoid scratches from the branches. Rose seized the opportunity, capturing the lead and maintained a short lead for the next kilometers.

In the final quarter of the race, Kaitlyn's perseverance at practice paid off. She went into a sprint, pulling on every ounce of strength left in her being, lungs burning, trails of clammy sweat dripping everywhere on her body.

Rose went into her own dash, but her stride could not keep up with Kaitlyn's. She went through the finish line, her family cheering along with her team mates.

She'd won! By a good two meters.

After a short recovery, Kaitlyn gave everyone a clammy hug. To her elation, even Josh Recollent from grade eleven came bounding up for a hug of his own. Her face still heat-flushed from the race likely turned a deep crimson when Josh hugged her, but she did her utmost to remain nonchalant.

Once all of the results had been compiled, Kaitlyn received a gold medal for her win. It was decided that the family would go out to an all-you-can-eat Chinese buffet to celebrate. During the meal, young Buck stared right at Kaitlyn, and in an irritating singsong voice, began to tease her. "Kaitlyn's got a boyfriend, Kaitlyn's got a boyfriend."

When Nathan chimed in, her mom stepped in to stop the harrassment. The more she interferred, the sillier and louder the boys became.

"Stop being so stupid!" Susan ordered the boys with a warning look that meant possible reprisals later.

"Who? Us?" More shrieks of laughter erupted.

"Yes, you. Now, smarten up. Look, there's a video game over there …."

Chapter Two

Having graduated from law school in the class of 1989, Maxine Swayman went out on job interviews, seeking a position as an articling clerk to start her new career as a lawyer. Many of her friends from her study group had already acquired jobs.

Richard was leaving the Toronto area, having scored a spot in a Crown Attorney's office in London, Ontario. Three others were going to work as articling law students throughout the Toronto area. When they learned that she had secured a first interview with the prominent Bay Street firm of Curzon, Horowitz, Hough, Lympany, and Hess, her friends showed jealousy, mentioning how beautiful the firm's quarters were. All wished aloud they could hold a position in such a beautiful old brownstone building in Toronto.

From her perspective, the Monday afternoon interview went really well. She believed she delivered an eloquent and well-crafted performance. Both Mr. Hough and Mr. Horowitz knew her father well.

It was never clear whether it was because of, or in spite of this fact that, the next day Maxine learned the position had been given to another incumbent. Granted, it had been her first interview, but nonetheless, she sank into a blue funk. Not even Nicola, her sister and roommate, could raise her spirits.

The following Friday evening in anticipation of a

planned gathering, Maxine put Billy Joel's beloved *Piano Man* on the stereo, mixed a pitcher of strawberry daiquiris, and set out corn chips, salsa, and guacamole on the veranda terrace.

Didi, Maxine's secondary school pal, and Samuel, a new friend from England, were due at the waterfront apartment within the hour. The evening plans involved cocktail hour with their guests, followed by dinner at *North of 49*, and a night of dancing in clubs.

Her preparations complete, Maxine lounged on the balcony, sipping on a diet soda and warming her body in the heat of the July sun as she admired the several yachts on the harbour criss-crossing the shimmering water like water beetles.

She sighed. It was a beautiful evening, but one shadowed by the fact that she was still jobless. She could rely on connections through her dad, however, she aimed at making it on her own merits.

The telephone rang, interrupting her mulling. She uncoiled herself from her chaise lounge and hurried inside.

"Maxine?" At her acknowledgement, the other party went on, "It's Uncle Stan. Congratulations on your graduation. Now that you're a lawyer, the family could use you." The man paused. She figured Stan was pooling on his courage to go on. "Can you come up north tonight or tomorrow?"

First, Maxine was astonished to hear from her father's second cousin of the Cummings side of the family. How was she even related to him? She didn't even know, but one fact remained: His voice was downright pushy and it irked her.

"Uncle Stan ... I haven't talked to you in ... over two years. What's happening? It sounds, uh, important ...." The anticipation of her evening dissipated like air gushing out from a balloon.

"I've got to call your dad more often. Here's the thing: Your cousin Stacey is due in criminal court on Monday. We need a lawyer who isn't from this Godforsaken little hick town to defend her."

Despite having met Stacey only a handful of times, Maxine was not surprised or concerned at this latest development. Stacey was a stuck-up little brat. "When was she arrested?"

"Two months ago."

Maxine bit her tongue, stiffening at the gall of the man. Then in true Swayman form she had inherited from her dad, she blurted out, "So why are you calling me the Friday before court?" Overhearing his deep intake of breath, she detected an embarrassment, a lengthy hesitation from him.

"I fired the last lawyer," he confirmed at last. "You'll be better. You're fresh out of school and, I'm sure, want to establish yourself professionally. I want you to take on the case."

She wondered what exactly had transpired that Stan had to resort to calling her, making Stacey's trouble with the law known to the entire family. "Why did you fire the last one?"

"He wanted my Stacey to plead guilty and take a plea bargain, like a common criminal. Could you believe that? Plus Stacey didn't relate well to the man. He even claimed that Stacey is a spoiled child who needs to grow up."

Maxine silently praised and agreed with the gutsy lawyer. Curiosity got the best of her. "What's she charged with?"

Stan's voice became hushed. "Well ... Personally, I think it was a girl's prank that went desperately wrong. Stacey fell under the influence of a no-good boy. Both went to an unchaperoned party together. A Native girl threatened my Stacey, and she retaliated by slipping LSD into her beer. You know those Indians; they're drunk all the time anyway."

The roundabout admission triggered a memory: why her dad hadn't spent much time with Stan over the years, and the hair on the back of her neck prickled uncomfortably.

As children, Nicola and her had always referred to Stan as their uncle even though he was only their father's second cousin. Stan Cummings was a successful businessman who bragged openly about locating his factory up north to avoid paying the workers a decent wage. She distinctly remembered how her father had then been horrified at his cousin's avarice.

Obviously expecting Maxine to jump at the chance at being in court, Stan pursued with his convincing argument when she remained silent on the matter. "The Indian girl was brought to the hospital by a male relation who told the cops where they had been that evening. The cops went to the premises to investigate, entering the house without a parent present. They searched the others and my Stacey looking for drugs. Only two people were arrested; Stacey and her boyfriend, Mike Smith."

"What is Stacey's take on all this, Uncle Stan?"

"She admits doing it. But only as a joke. Stacey claims this Native, one of those rough types living on a reservation without toilets, has goaded her for years. The girl is ... fatherless as well."

In light of the obvious discrimination going on, she wouldn't take the case. "Uncle Stan, you'd better get another lawyer, not me. Or Dad."

"Listen, Maxine." Her Uncle Stan's voice took on a nasty edge, as if he were talking to an errant mill-hand. "I'm giving you the break of your life time, and you're throwing it away? Without even talking to your cousin? What's the problem?"

"Ethics."

"Huh?"

"Ethics, I said." The prospect of impending verbal combat flushed her cheeks.

"I don't get it."

Maxine slammed her hand on the desk at Stan's ignorance.

"Uncle Stan, I've just been called to the bar. I spent three months in criminal court as a law student. Doing menial work that lawyers typically assign to students. All

I got to do was assign court dates for the lawyers. I didn't do any real legal work.

"Secondly, Stacey is guilty, and even though she is a minor, a criminal record will adversely affect her. If I defend her, and it goes badly, there'll be tension in the family. Finally, your attitude toward the victim is completely prejudicial. Stacey could have murdered this Native girl, do you realize that?"

"I'm calling your father," Stan snapped, and the line went dead.

Maxine put the receiver back, and trying to calm down, she gulped on her soda. On a whim, she changed the current CD to a compilation of dance tunes, hoping that her fun night out with friends wouldn't be ruined by her mulling over Stan's phone call.

Just then, Nicola entered the apartment. She helped herself to a strawberry daiquiri. Following a sip, she sighed loudly, obviously at the marvellous effect the cool drink had on her. She turned to Maxine, a worried look overtaking her relaxed facial expression. "You look really pissed off. What's up?"

"Uncle Stan called. Took me a moment to realize who he was. He wants me to represent Stacey in a criminal suit." Maxine related the conversation she'd just had with their uncle, and finally shrugging, she ended with, "Dad hardly ever talks about him."

"Can you blame him?"

"I remember how Dad's attitude showed his dislike for the way Stan bragged about ripping off workers, paying them just above the poverty line. How Dad openly hated how Uncle Stan disliked the Natives living on a First Nation Territory near his home. I have a feeling there's a lot more to his dislike, though."

"Refill your drink, sis, and meet me on the terrace." Maxine did as she was told, then settled across from her sister.

"You're right. Dad and Uncle Stan were friendly enough while in University together. Dad took law and Uncle Stan took commerce. I think they belonged to the same frat house even.

"After university, they went their separate ways. Stan started his manufacturing plant. It was all a big success story, and he was making tons of money. Whenever he drove down to Toronto on business, he'd stop by for a visit. Dad tried to ignore his bigoted comments, until one day …. You remember Benton Carter from Dad's firm?"

"Of course, we practically grew up with his daughters."

"Benton stopped by one day when Uncle Stan and Dad were having drinks in the sun porch. On being introduced to one another, Stan refused to shake his hand. You know how proud Benton is."

Maxine nodded. "What an ignorant jerk."

"Dad was shocked by Stan's behaviour, but didn't let on, chatting with Benton while he led the man to his home office to discuss the legal matter that had brought Benton over. The poor man quickly left after they concluded their business. Dad marched back to the sun porch to rejoin Stan who said something like, 'Did some do-gooders force you to hire that … that ….' "

Nicola clamped her mouth shut and shook her head with sadness. She let out a huge sigh. "I can't even use the 'N' word to re-tell the story. Stan had crossed the line with Dad, insulting a good family friend. Dad's emotions just boiled over, and he lost it, ordering Stan to get the hell out of his house while he furiously added that Stan was no longer welcome. It was a real blood-bath …."

Maxine smiled broadly. She reached for a corn chip and dipped it into the salsa, now satisfied that the matter was closed. "Dad may hang up on him when Stan calls to complain about me." She sighed in renewed delight. "My night out might not get ruined after all."

Nicola turned to her with a don't-be-so-sure look. "Dad may look at it as a good opportunity for you. He may even send Benton to that little town to coach you. Now, wouldn't that be a joke?"

They shared a moment of laughter then Maxine

added on a serious note, "Dad wouldn't do that to a friend."

"I know. Just kidding." The phone rang, and they both stared at it ominously.

Maxine answered it and mouthed Dad to her sister. She went on to concentrate on her father's words, her spirits falling as she put her father on the speaker-phone.

"Maxine, I know you don't think much of Uncle Stan."

"Neither do you!"

"Be nice. Anyway, if your grandmother were alive she'd expect me to help our family. It's what families do."

Maxine sighed, loud enough for her dad to hear it. "I don't have trial experience."

"I'll act as second chair for you. It'll be fun."

"Dad, have you lost it? How is defending a bigot supposed to be fun?"

Overhearing her dad's persuasive words Nicola blurted, "Fun?" She let out a burst of laughter and slumped into the sofa, shaking her head at the turn of events.

"Think about it, you're getting your feet wet as a lawyer in a rinky-dink town where no one knows you. Plus it will look terrific on a resume. How many in your graduating class will be able to try a case?"

"Yeah, most are carrying the briefcases of the trial lawyers." She spared a look at Nicola and narrowed her eyes in warning.

"That's not good enough for my daughter, a second generation Swayman lawyer."

"Dad."

"Don't dad me. I'll pick you up on—"

"Dad, you're a tax lawyer."

"Sunday at seven." His tone indicated a finality. Maxine knew all was lost. "Trust me, I know my way around a courtroom. The toughest part of this trial will be putting up with my idiot cousin."

"Fine."

"See you then."

* * * *

Maxine brooded while her dad drove into the small Georgian Bay community at eleven, Sunday morning. They stopped at a side road restaurant and grabbed an early lunch of hot roast beef dipped sandwiches with a side order of hand-cut fries. Any delay to reaching Stan Cummings' home was a God send to her

They quickly got back on the road, and Maxine decided she quite liked the little town, especially the way the roads wound and corkscrewed through verdant corridors of bush country. When they finally pulled into the driveway of the spacious log home, the scent of lilac bushes and pine trees was a refreshing change from smog-filled Toronto. She opened the car door, and a heat wave assaulted her. She stepped into the gravelled driveway, little tiny beads of sweat already forming on her brow.

Her father marched up to the front door of the home with her close on his heel. Stan Cummings opened the massive wooden door and cuffed his cousin lovingly on the shoulder. Maxine didn't miss how her father's skin on his neck reddened, and how he pulled brusquely away from Stan.

A blond girl wearing cotton-candy pink track pants with striped leg warmers took a position next to Stan.

Stan hooked a loving arm around Stacey's shoulders. "You remember your cousin, don't you, Maxine?"

Maxine nodded to Stacey with reservation. "We were pretty young the last time we saw each other."

The fourteen-year-old gave her a curt wave. "Yeah, cousin, and now you're the lawyer and I'm the criminal," Stacey mocked openly.

Ungrateful little bitch was Maxine's first thought. If it weren't professional suicide, she'd throw the damn case and let her stew in a correction facility for a bit. Do her some good.

Stan dropped his arm from Stacey's shoulders to wave them ahead through a large foyer. "Stacey, behave. This is not the time for sarcasm, Maxine is here to get you out of this unpleasantness." He turned to his guests. "Through the double door and watch your step, Harvey."

Maxine spied an open concept diningroom with the kitchen to the right. The interior of the Cummings' home, a log cabin with fourteen-foot walls, was spacious. Though beautiful, it lacked character, resembling a show home from a design magazine. No family pictures adorned walls. It lacked warmth. It was only for show.

The four of them settled in the sunken living room with its vaulted ceiling, her dad and herself choosing to sit side by side. Each of them pulled out pads of legal paper, then Maxine turned to Stacey. "What can you tell us about this incident, Stacey?"

"For the last eight years or so, this skanky Indian girl has been getting on my nerves. First, she won a speech contest, then we were forced to listen to her as our Valedictorian at our grade eight graduation, and now she's accusing me of this nonsense.

"Anyway, that night, she was chugging back the beers, her type does that every night, you know, and I slipped some acid in her drink as a joke. I figured she'd get a buzz and we'd laugh—"

"What were you thinking?" Maxine blurted out, incensed by the lack of remorse from Stacey.

"I told you – her type likes the drugs and the alcohol, I figured she could handle it." In her careless attitude, her cousin heaved her shoulders. "I had no idea this was her first trip on acid. As a matter of fact, this kind of shocked me."

Maxine stared her cousin down. "Kind of shocks me too. She could have died." Her usually professional delivery resonated with anger. What a business her father had dragged her into. This was, trying to defend the indefensible!

41

"You're just as dramatic as my dad," blustered Stacey. "They pumped her stomach, and if that cousin of hers had kept his mouth shut, the cops would never have come to the party and arrested me. I'm working on getting him kicked off the football team."

Maxine shook her head in disgust. Getting through to that girl was as hopeless as expecting global warming to stop. Stacey harboured no personal responsibility.

"Stacey, I don't think you're taking this matter at all seriously," Harvey Swayman said gravely.

"I've got two Toronto lawyers and I'm a minor," Stacey said smugly. "I may have to do volunteer work for a year. Otherwise, I'm scot-free."

Maxine grasped her dad's arm; she could feel her green eyes flaring with ill-suppressed anger. "Stacey," she started. After heaving a huge breath she carried on, "The fact that we are from Toronto may or may not work in your favour. Small towns usually prefer their own lawyers and do not take kindly to outsiders. Also, because you have two legal counsels, the judge may think you have something even greater to hide than the drugging. Now, just quit with the teenage attitude and smarten up. You could have killed someone's child and you're treating this whole situation like it will go away without a doubt."

Stacey Cummings' eyes glassed over and one tiny tear escaped her reddened eyes. Evidently, the girl never had anyone talk to her as though she were less than perfect.

"It's okay, Stacey," Uncle Stan said soothingly, and Maxine bristled.

Go ahead, Stan, make me look like a self-righteous goody two-shoes.

Her uncle turned to her with a pleading look. "She's just a teen, Maxine. She didn't mean to hurt her classmate. It was just a prank. Plead it out to mischief, please? I beg you. I don't even want Stacey in criminal court."

Maxine spared a questioning glance at her father.

At his encouraging nod, she settled into her lawyer mode, undaunted by her uncle's tactics to soften her approach. "Where's the Crown's screening form?" she asked Stan.

He produced the document, passing it to her dad. Nonplussed, Maxine leaned into her dad's side and read it aloud. "The charge is assault causing bodily harm. The Crown Attorney's office is asking for two years probation, one hundred hours community service, and psychological counselling."

In her thinking mode, Maxine ran her fingers through her hair. "I might be able to get the Crown to reduce the charge to assault without the bodily harm since the girl recovered; however, probation, community service hours, and the counselling will have to stay."

Stacey leaped to her feet. "Screw this! Why do I need counselling?"

Maxine prompted her dad. "You'd better answer this one." She settled back into the couch, her body humming with tension.

"Stacey, you are a young woman with a lot of promise; however, as the child of a prominent citizen ..." Harvey paused as if to find the right words that would reach the teen. He added in a sombre tone, "you have shown childish judgment. I suspect your parents have given you every luxury, and instead of embracing your opportunities, you are squandering them. You don't appreciate the seriousness of your actions. And if you don't smarten up now, you will be heading toward a lifetime of trouble. Whether you realize it or not, your present actions are a forecast of future performance. You're fourteen-years-old and already into heavy drugs. I know how intelligent you dad is...." Overhearing Maxine's stifle a chuckle, he paused.

"I know that you have promise. But so far, you're throwing your opportunities away. You have no remorse whatsoever. A counsellor will help you realize why you are acting so recklessly." Her dad took a breath to add something else then, as if suddenly realizing that Stacey still stared at the vaulted ceiling in no apparent hurry to gain from his talk, he changed his mind.

Stacey didn't regain any eye contact for the rest of the meeting. She radiated the hostility of defensiveness.

Maxine turned her attention to Stan. "I'll call the Crown Attorney tomorrow morning and find out what she is willing to negotiate. I may be able to get the probation reduced to one year, from two. If all goes well, we'll go to court on Tuesday and plead it out. If we can't agree, we'll set a court date for further down the road. Who knows, it may even be all over by Tuesday."

Chapter Three

At 6 am, Kaitlyn Wolfe awoke in her room and the first thing she saw was a picture of her father. The late OPP Constable Clarence Wolfe posing in his dress uniform looked stunning to her. Then her glance fell on the four medallions earned through elementary school speech contests. Thoughts of what the day had in store of her came next, crowding her mind.

Without the support of her beloved father who had passed away last July, she would face her abuser in court, a racist that had nearly murdered her back in October. Rousting herself from bed, she began to weep uncontrollably.

Kaitlyn showered and mentally went over the Assistant Crown Attorney's instructions. Debra Watson was a kind woman who had made her comfortable. Ms. Watson needed her presence at Stacey's trial, in case Kaitlyn was called as a witness.

Her mother peeked in her room, "Are you ready?"

"Do my clothes look okay?" Kaitlyn pulled the final zipper of her outfit and picked up a brush to quickly set her long black hair.

"You look fine, sweety." Her mom smiled, came to her and hugged her tightly.

"Then I guess so."

They said their goobyes to the babysitter for Nathan and got in the station wagon. The women drove from

45

Wanitou into the town of Harrisville in silence.

Of medium size, Harrisville hosted all the trials for two First Nations communities and six small hamlets. Her mother eased the vehicle into the parking lot of the Provincial Courthouse. Kaitlyn's nervousness increased ten-fold.

"Mom? I'm scared," Kaitlyn revealed between quiet sobs. Her mother reached out to her and squeezed her hand.

"I would be too, Katie." Her mom's voice was soft and emotional. Then she turned her attention to parking the station wagon. Once she turned the ignition off, she gave Kaitlyn a meaningful glance. "Remember you're the victim and that spoilt girl is going to pay for nearly killing you."

"We've been over what I should expect a thousand times, but look at this huge building! Creepy people are entering it."

Her mother gave her a look of warning. "Shame on you. Many of these people may be criminals, but many are victims of circumstance. Hold your head high, and we'll show our family's dignity. Don't be afraid. I'm here with you."

Still choking on sobs, Kaitlyn admitted, "If I hadn't listened to Susan, I would never have snuck out of the house that night."

Her mother gave her a smile that warmed her, soothed her. "Kids make mistakes. I've long since forgiven you. Now, let's get ready for the case."

One last squeeze of the hand from her mother and they exited the car, heading toward a side entrance of the courthouse. Kaitlyn pointed out to her mom the official sign that listed three courtrooms on the second floor. They took the stairs and sat in the hallway between the courtrooms. The wooden bench was stiff and uncomfortable.

Fifteen minutes later, Stacey and her entourage emerged from the stairwell. Stacey's father, Stan – a well known, but disliked businessman – her mother Kari, and two strangers strolled toward the courthouses' doors.

Of the two strangers, first was a woman in her twenties, wearing a taupe business suit with shoulder pads, gorgeous red hair with Mediterranean green eyes which matched her outfit so perfectly. The grey-haired man followed close behind. He was the epitomy of confidence with his Gianni Versace black dress-shoes and black pinstriped suit. Kaitlyn grew even more nervous than before.

A quiet Stacey Cummings trailed behind. Her customary arrogance undetectable because of her terrified look. Kaitlyn despised the girl for the trouble and pain she'd caused her. Although still very angry at Stacey, Kaitlyn pulled out a biology textbook, and avoided eye contact with her enemy.

Her mom leaned into her. "Those people must be her legal representation," she whispered. "They're *not* from Harrisville."

"No, they're not. During a recess, I overheard Stacey gloat that she's got lawyers from Toronto. Apparently, the team consists of six of them, but it looks like only two came along."

Her mom cocked her head to get a better look. "Don't be so sure. The red-haired woman looks young, she may be a secretary. Now, the older man may very well be the lawyer."

"Mom?" Kaitlyn asked with a hint of hesitation. "Who do I have on my side?"

Margaret sighed. "You have the truth, the police, the crown attorney and me. Stacey has a good smoke screen, but you'll be fine."

"I'd better study."

Three boys, known troublemakers from her school, strutted with bravado as though they believed that being in trouble with the law was a badge of honour. She tried to concentrate on her book as they entered courtroom one, sparing an evil grin at her.

What losers! Over her texbook she then spotted

Bucky, the vagrant who habitually sat in front of the convenience store. He'd dressed up today in a tattered brown suit and running shoes.

Stacey's group stopped short of the entrance of courtroom one, roughly twenty feet from Kaitlyn and her mom, and began an exchange.

"Stacey, you'll have to stand up in court and admit to your actions." Kaitlyn overheard the instructions of the redhaired woman, and her interest was picked.

"I've spoken to the Crown Attorney. If you admit your involvement, she'll ..."

Two men involved in a heated discussion walked by and stifled the din from Stacey's group. Kaitlyn strained to hear but it was no use.

As if there had been a signal, the crowd outside the courtroom began filing in twenty minutes before the proceedings were scheduled to begin. Youths were shufflling, grown-ups slouched and one particular lady rushed in, notebook in hand.

Stacey spared a glare at Kaitlyn then followed the others in.

"Mom, why can't I go in and listen to the proceedings?"

Margaret smiled to reassure her. "Remember what Ms. Watson said: As a witness you can't go in until your name is called over the loud speaker."

"It's wrong. Stacey could be lying in there. She's good at that."

Her mom acknowledged the Assistant Crown Attorney with a nod as Ms. Watson wheeled a file box into the courtroom, sparing an encouraging smile at Kaitlyn and a warning, "I'll be right back."

Debra Watson returned promptly and guided Kaitlyn and her mom into a private room, a law library across the hall from the courtroom. A headache was creeping in on Kaitlyn.

"Please sit. I tried to call your home last night but the line was busy."

"Regarding?" Margaret asked with surprise.

"I had a meeting with Stacey's lawyer, Maxine Swayman. After considerable deliberations, I'm going to accept a plea bargain from Stacey. Kaitlyn, do you know what a plea bargain is?"

"No."

"It's a negotiation where the accused, in this case Ms.Cummings, admits to a crime. In order to save the expense of a trial, I accept plea bargains. I only accept a plea bargain if it's reasonable and if it spares the victim some pain."

"So, she'll admit to puting LSD in my beer?"

"Ms. Cummings will be convicted of assault for drugging you."

A confused look came over her mom. "What about the assault causing bodily harm that we talked about in our meeting?"

"It's been reduced."

"That young woman tried to kill my only daughter and her charge is reduced!" Margaret shook her head. "Unacceptable."

"Mrs. Wolfe, our police have gone over the evidence. We have no proof that Stacey Cummings meant to kill Kaitlyn. Unfortunately, it was a cruel teenage prank that went desperately wrong. If I tried the case for assault causing bodily harm, Ms. Cummings might get no punishment at all. With the plea bargain, she will be on probation and our officers will keep an eye on her."

"If we were rich, would the playing field be any different?" Margaret asked with a reserved put-out tone.

Debra Watson gave her mom a meaningful glance. "I assure you, I'd try the case the same way, regardless of social status of the people involved. I'm sorry that you don't agree with me, Mrs. Wolfe." Ms. Watson turned to Kaitlyn. "You have a choice. You can now watch the sentencing which may give closure or you can go back to school and put the incident behind you." She stood up. "I've got to get to court."

"I don't agree with your decision, Ms. Watson. It

makes me angry and irritated." Kaitlyn glared at the Assistant Crown Attorney. "I'll watch Stacey's plea bargain unfold."

The attorney left the room, and Margaret leaped at Kaitlyn then hugged her, tears streaming down her face. "It's not fair, it's not fair. She's a spoilt brat, who tried to kill you, and she's getting a slap on the wrist."

"I don't like it either, mom, but I won't let her ruin me. I'm glad I voiced my displeasure to Ms. Watson." Kaitlyn felt her shoulders become taut as she lifted her head high. "If Daddy was alive he'd expect me to be strong. Mom, I'll tell you right now, that air-head isn't going to destroy me, and I won't give away my power to her."

"I love you so much, Kailtyn. You're a brave girl." Margaret smiled, winked, then nodded toward the courtroom. "Let's get a seat."

They entered the room filled with long benches that reminded Kaitlyn of pews in a church. They chose to sit about halfway back from the front row. At the front of the courtroom was a raised platform with a large desk with a coat of arms adorning the wall above it. She assumed it would be where the judge held court. She quickly became engrossed into each action, each minute detail that could be spotted inside the courtroom.

Ms. Watson stacked her files on a dark stained wooden table that faced the platform. Another long table beside hers, likely the prosecutor's table for the defense lawyer, sat empty for now. Despite the benches filled to capacity in the main part of the court, the room oozed a cold aura. Kaitlyn shivered at the ominous setting.

Glancing around, she caught sight of Mr. Campbell, a lawyer who used to chitchat with her dad during her field hockey games. His daughter, Trina, was on the team. Kaitlyn recognized the court services officer as well.

Leaning over to her mom, she whispered, "It's going to be a long day. I'd rather be in school."

Her mom reached for her hand and squeezed.

"Honey, I'd rather you were in school and that none of this had happened."

Kaitlyn recognized Stacey and her group settled in the second row. Stacey was looking around also, sparing a long look at Bucky while ensuring she didn't have any eye contact with him. Then her gaze moved about, catching Kaitlyn's presence. She rolled her eyes but Kaitlyn maintained her stare at her abuser.

The older man, probably Stacey's lawyer, and the pretty lady left the bench to take up position in the area reserved for lawyers. Kaitlyn resumed assimilating their every move.

At a small commotion, Stacey turned around. She did as well.

The three boys from school had taken seats at the very back of the courtroom. They were grinning and snickering at her as the proceedings were about to begin.

Thirty minutes into the session, Stacey's name was called over the loudspeaker. Stacey rose and took a couple of steps, already at the front of the court. Kaitlyn stifle a laugh. It was evident to her that Stacey didn't know where to stand. At an inviting gesture from her lawyer, Stacey took an empty place beside them.

The redhaired lawyer stood and addressed the judge. "Your Honour, I'm Maxine Swayman, S W A Y M A N, initial M. I'm representing Ms. Cummings in this matter."

The suavely dressed older man stood up and said, "Your Honour, I'm Harvey Swayman, same spelling, and I'm serving second chair to Ms. Swayman."

Kaitlyn caught the young woman stealing a smile toward the older man. She assumed Ms. Swayman to be his daughter.

The Judge, a serious-looking grey-haired man, nodded his head in acknowledgement to the introductions.

A horrible spitting sound echoed throughout the room, startling all present, who turned, seeking for the dreadful cause.

Just then the vagrant fell forward, crumpling onto the floor. Bucky began convulsing and writhing. The court services officer leaped forward to help. Once he reached Bucky, he held him as still as possible.

The Judge rose from his chair to get a better look at the commotion. After a eyeful, he turned to his bailiff. "Call an ambulance and clear the courtroom."

Over forty people were rushed out of the courtroom. Kaitlyn and her mom took the remaining unoccupied seats in the long hallway. Stacey exited with her lawyers and her parents in tow. She slipped another glare at Kaitlyn, but to no avail. Kaitlyn wouldn't give her the satisfaction and held her head high, acting as if Stacey weren't even there.

Soon, ambulance attendants were rushing out of the courtroom with their patient secured on the gurney. The vagrant wore an oxygen mask and looked grotesquely pale and sickly.

"That's old Bucky, the junkie, he's probably wasted again," remarked a bystander.

Kaitlyn's attention was commanded by Stacey's screech.

Stacey was leaping off the wooden bench she'd just taken. Kaitlyn looked on, puzzled as her nemesis beelined toward the bathroom, to be nearly run over by the ambulance gurney whooshing by. As though unaware of having been nearly run over, Stacey ran into the ladies' room, still pulling the rear of her dress up front as if trying to hide the evident wet spot. Kaitlyn tried to suppress her laughter, but in vain.

Oh, how the mighty have fallen.

A few minutes later, Stacey returned to her mom's side. Kaitlyn overheard her whining. "Someone had peed on the bench – the smell was so disgusting, can I go home now?" Stacey asked, while sobbing likely out of frustration.

"Control yourself, Stacey," her mother stated in a frank voice. Stacey whimpered but managed to regain as much composure as she could for the return to court.

Court reconvened moments later and Stacey's name was called once again.

Kaitlyn felt a bit of sympathy for Stacey. She was having such a terrible day.

Debra Watson, the Assistant Crown Attorney, addressed the judge. "Even though this is a first appearance, the accused, Ms. Cummings, would like to enter a plea to a lesser charge of assault under section 266 of the criminal code."

The Judge turned to Stacey. "Ms. Cummings, please stand." Stacey complied. "You stand accused of assaulting another woman named Kaitlyn Wolfe on October 3, 1982. How do you plead?"

After a hesitation, Stacey managed, "Guilty, Your Honour."

The judge's brow knitted together. "Ms. Cummings, speak up."

This time, Stacey produced her words in a louder, clearer voice. "Guilty, Your Honour." At her answer, the judge gave a curt nod.

"In accepting this plea, you will have a criminal record. Do you understand this?"

"Yes, sir," she squeaked.

Kaitlyn was unsure if Stacey knew of all the repercussions. By the ominous stare of the Judge, she was sure that Stacey would soon find out.

"Young lady, I've read the entire report, and for a fourteen-year-old, your conduct was nothing less than horrible. Drugs ruin lives, and this may be your only chance to turn your life around." Still glaring at her, he nodded in the direction of her parents. "I see your parents are here to support you. I sincerely hope that you smarten up and get the counselling you need to clean up your life before it becomes a nightmare." The Judge's voice had risen to a thunderous volume, echoing throughout the courtroom.

He must hate Stacey for what she did to me.

Finally, he let up on Stacey to turn to Ms. Watson.

Jacqui Morrison

"Do you want a sentencing report, Ms. Watson?"

"No, sir. I'm prepared to enter the negotiated terms into the record: Ms. Cummings will abstain from alcohol and drugs; she will be on probation for twelve months; complete one hundred hours of community service as directed by her probation officer; receive counselling, meet with a probation officer monthly, keep the peace and be of good behaviour."

The Judge shifted his gaze to Stacey. "Do you understand these conditions, Ms. Cummings?"

"Yes, sir," Stacey admitted.

Despite her admission, Kaitlyn surmised that Stacey was likely already trying to figure a way to wiggle out of some community service.

"Good. Young lady, for your sake, I hope I don't see you in my courtroom again." With those words, the Judge closed the file on his bench. Stacey's gaze fell to the floor. Her reddened neck and slouched appearance had Kaitlyn realizing that the popular girl looked cheap and defeated.

Their group left their place to make room for the next accused as another name was called from what appeared to be a lengthy roster as per the crowded room.

As they walked toward the exit, Stacey's legal counsel, spoke up. "I know the Judge may have sounded harsh, Stacey," she said, "but he's trying to save you from a life of drugs and turmoil. You don't want to end up like that poor guy they dragged out of there."

Kaitlyn's mother chose that moment to rise from her seat to also exit the courtroom. Kaitlyn followed suit. Their action was caught by Stacey's lawyer who momentarily stopped her lecture. Stacey bristled.

Moving through the waiting room, Kaitlyn noted Stacey glaring at her own lawyer who had just finished saying, "You don't want to end up like old Bucky, do you?"

"Maxine," Stan Cummings cut in, "this is a bit harsh. Think about everything poor Stacey has been through."

Kaitlyn's brow arched in stunned anger.

The woman lawyer stopped dead in her tracks. "Stan. Every day, I think about poor Kaitlyn who could have died if that boy hadn't gotten her to the hospital in time. May I remind you that when I first interviewed Stacey, she wanted that boy kicked off the football team." With flushed cheeks, the lawyer resumed her walking, looking insulted and adding over her shoulder, "What Stacey doesn't realize just yet, is that if Kaitlyn's cousin hadn't got her to the hospital, Stacey might have been facing a manslaughter trial and not an assault charge."

Kaitlyn followed behind the others, truly shocked at what could have happened to Stacey, if ....

Stacey relented. "Thanks for being there for me, Maxine. I'll follow the conditions. Honest."

"All I can say, Stacey, is pay attention to what the Judge said, and smarten up. If you work hard and sincerely commit to counselling, you may eventually get pardoned from this conviction."

"Pardoned?" Stacey's father cut in. "My daughter is a young offender, I thought those records were sealed?"

The older lawyer explained, "Yes, they are sealed, but the police forces in Ontario have access to them, and if Stacey is stopped for even a traffic ticket, they will deem her to be a violent person. The police may treat her roughly because of this conviction. Your daughter was just convicted of a crime of violence."

Chapter Four

While her father drove his BMW out of Harrisville and onto the 400 South heading back to Toronto, Maxine couldn't help remembering how tall and proud the victim had been. She so resented Stan and Stacey for their racism. "I never want to see those relatives again!" she blurted, out of sheer frustration.

"I couldn't agree more." He chuckled. "I must admit it did my heart proud sitting beside my attorney daughter in court."

"God, I was shaking the whole time."

"Well, my dear, you have that Swayman self-assurance because no one noticed your uneasiness. What you said about Stacey turning out like that unfortunate vagrant was poorly phrased, but still appropriate. Essentially, you got your cousin off with a slap on the wrist and, unless she feels sincere remorse, she'll get nowhere. It'll just be the same old thing all over again. You gave her another chance. Now it's up to her to make something of it."

* * * *

Three weeks after Stacey's trial, Maxine began her tenure at the law firm of Stern, Perlman, Heifetz, and Zukerman.

A dream job, it was not.

What followed was a truly miserable six months. The senior lawyer, to whom she was assigned to, had little interest in her capabilities. He expected her to carry briefcases and file boxes, and perform other menial chores.

Visiting her parents, she vented to her dad once their spaghetti dinner was finished. "I went to law school for this?" Maxine shook her head in sour disappointment and pouted. "This job is an absolute bore."

"I can sympathize with how you feel," her dad commiserated, "considering you were top of your class, it must be frustrating."

She grabbed a sweet tidbit from the plate her mom had just centered on the kitchen table and chomped into it. She quickly swallowed to add, "I have so much more to offer to the firm."

"Kiddo, stick with it and spend your free time looking for internal positions within the law firm, or externally if you have to."

"Good idea, Dad."

* * * *

A few months later, Maxine started shopping for a job in another firm.

However, an opportunity came her way within the present firm to work with a senior lawyer who practiced predominantly family law for wealthy clients. She accepted the post.

Heather Taylor was a true professional, who took a genuine interest in her, grooming her for success. Maxine felt the chemistry between them was completely natural and spontaneous.

On a Monday morning, Heather approached Maxine at her desk. "Good morning."

Maxine dropped her work and welcomed Heather with a smile.

"Regan Johnston in the criminal division is short-staffed for the next month. His junior lawyer broke his leg skiing."

Maxine grimaced. "Ouch!"

"Ouch is right. The poor guy's in traction with a compound fracture. You've been reassigned to Regan's staff."

"What about your work?" Maxine asked.

"You've done such a thorough job that I'm in good shape. Just don't let Regan steal you forever."

"Ha! As if I would allow this. When do I go over to the other side?"

"After lunch, I'm afraid."

Maxine reported to Regan's office to be diverted to the courthouse on University Avenue, near Toronto City Hall, for a set-court date.

Regan filled her in on the basics. "I have six case files. I need you to find the defendants, who've pleaded not guilty, and introduce yourself."

She nodded her understanding.

"When their names are called, you stand up for them. The judge will suggest hearing dates. Double-check my availability in my agenda then confirm or negotiate alternative dates. Honey Loupier, the socialite, won't be appearing; you'll stand up for her as well."

She gave him a stupefied look. "The heir to the Loupier Chocolate firm?"

"One in the same," he said with a curt nod.

"Do tell ...."

"I don't know how much you know about socialites but most of them are spoilt brats. About a year ago, she went into Horbath's Jewelry on Eglinton and wanted a tennis bracelet. The clerk ran her credit card but the purchase was declined."

"Declined! For a Loupier heir?"

Maxine caught the pronounced raised of Regan's eyebrow. "It was a $10,000 bracelet. Need I say more?"

Maxine mouthed the amount in utter shock.

"Ms. Loupier apparently confronted the clerk with a 'Don't you know who I am?' The clerk confirmed she did.

"Honey Loupier then snatched the bracelet from the

clerk and ordered, 'Then bill my Dad,' and walked out. The storeowner called the cops, and Honey was arrested."

Maxine stifled a giggle, unsure of whether or not she should be laughing in front of her new supervisor.

"Maxine. You can let go; the laughter I mean. It's a hilarious story. Her father gives her $10,000 a month from her trust fund, and Honey doesn't like to budget." He shrugged as if to end the tale. "She won't be at the set-court date."

Regan handed Maxine the associated files, concluding their meeting. She took them, flashing him with a warm smile. She rose, settled the files on the crook of her left arm, and left his office with an I'll-do-my-best parting note.

The set-court date was a breeze. Five male clients had been charged with white-collar crimes. All were polite to Maxine. She confidently stood up each time the defendant's name was called and did exactly what Regan required of her.

Over the next two weeks, Regan had her do similar appearances at two other courts in Toronto. On a Friday afternoon, he popped by her cubicle and asked with a mischevious demeanor, "Do you want to have some fun?"

His hazel eyes were animated, full of mischief. The temptation was too great, she nodded.

"Monday at 10 a.m. you get yourself in the conference room, for a meeting … with Honey Loupier."

"Really?" Regan's anticipation was infectious. "What do you need me to do?"

"Heather told me a bit about your upbringing, which I understand is similar to Honey's. You will be there to pull her back to earth if she tries her arrogant nonsense during the meeting."

Unsure whether she shared any arrogance or non-sense with Honey, she warned her supervisor. "I did go to private schools, but my parents didn't name me after an ingredient."

Regan slapped the desk, bursting out laughing. "Good one!"

* * * *

On Monday at 9:55 a.m. Regan and Maxine entered the boardroom of Stern, Perlman, Heifetz, and Zukerman and settled in at the mahogany table where ten other leather chairs remained unused.

Their wait for Ms. Loupier's arrival was brightened by a familiar face, a jovial secretary who set up tea and coffee prepped using a silver tea set. Worth thousands of dollars, Maxine surmised.

Ms. Loupier breezed in forty-five minutes late in a black party dress, wafting Chanel Number 5 fragance throughout the room. Her frosted hair looked chaotic and her make-up looked slept in.

"Let's get this little misunderstanding over with," she commanded in a voice as smooth as a television star. She slumped in the nearest chair into her.

Regan, who had stood at her entrance like a gentleman, offered, "Coffee, Ms. Loupier." Maxine rose to serve. She had waited to serve herself for as long as she could, but on the second occasion the secretary refreshed the pot, she had foregone her manners.

Honey Loupier glanced at the credenza devoid of anything but the serving silver set. "Only if you have a shot of bourbon to strengthen it."

Maxine changed her mind and sat back down, her action not even qualifying for a glance from Ms. Loupier.

Regan glared at Honey, the coffee offer forgotten. "I've spoken to the Crown Attorney. Since this is your first criminal offence, he's prepared to offer you a conditional discharge."

Honey narrowed her gaze at him. "What in the hell is that?"

Regan heaved an appeasing breath as if he'd already lost patience with his client. "Basically, you'll have twelve months to stay out of trouble with the law.

Once the twelve months is up, the conviction will go away from your record. Some conditions will be set though."

Honey's lower jaw could have hit the table. She seemed livid that conditions would apply. However, she quickly recovered with a retort. "I haven't done anything wrong."

Maxine cleared her throat on purpose. Having gained Honey's full attention, she reminded Ms. Loupier, "You walked out of a jewellery store with a $10,000 bracelet. One you didn't pay for."

The socialite's eyes could have shot daggers. "Who do you think ...." Her eyes brightened in recognition. "You're Maxine ... from that private school I attended for a semester. You were a brainiac."

Maxine acknowledged with a curt not and reached over the table to shake Honey's hand. But Honey was already sending her air kisses on both cheeks.

Mentally shaking her head, Maxine settled back down her chair, then went into a legal explaination. "Mr. Johnston here has negotiated you a sweetheart of a deal. If it were anyone else other than you, they'd be in jail for theft over $5,000. An indictable offence."

She went on, reaching for a document from the file, "All you have to comply with is a mere fifty hours of community service, report to a probation officer monthly and attend whatever counselling the probation officer deems necessary. Once the year is up, as long as you don't do anything imprudent, you'll walk away without a record."

"But Maxine, Daddy would have paid for it."

"The proper procedure under the circumstance was to have the clerk contact your father on the spot to get approval. Or ... fill out a credit application like anyone else." Maxine paused, giving Honey an I-mean-it look. "You're not above the law despite how well off you are."

Regan, who during their exchange had gotten himself a cup of coffee and was returning to his seat, nearly spat out a mouthful of coffee in a burst of shock mixed with laughter.

But Honey had only eyes for Maxine now. "I see your point, Maxine, but that means, I won't be able to go skiing in Vale this winter."

Maxine took a calming breath. "My way, means that you won't be strip searched by guards and suffer more unpleasanteries. I'm strongly advising you to take the deal."

Dubious, Honey gave her a questioning look. "They strip search you?"

Maxine gravely acknowledged. "The moment you enter prison and whenever they feel it is necessary there after."

"Crap!"

"Honey, you wouldn't do well in prison. Heck, I wouldn't do well in prison. None of us that went to Fenton Hall would. The inmates will hate you because you're wealthy; meanwhile, the guards won't give a darn about you. If this goes to trial and you lose, prison will be where you'll end up, no doubt in my mind."

"I'll take the deal." Honey reached for the pen and paper that Maxine had suggestively pushed in her direction.

"Good thinking, Ms. Loupier." Regan gave Maxine a look of approval.

* * * *

Her time with Regan came to an end, and interesting as the work was with Heather, Maxine found out her true calling to be criminal law.

She excelled at it because most people didn't intimidate her, but she had the presence of mind to choose her battles well. In a short time, Maxine ended up as an associate for the firm with very high billable hours, and those turned out as a great deal of money for the firm and herself.

Life was good and getting better.

Three years after working for Stern, Perlman,

Heifetz, and Zukerman, she opened her own firm on Gloucester Street thanks to her benevolent father who provided financing. It was all due to her natural ability and her need for autonomy.

Three doors down the road from her new office were ram-shackle, run-down rooming houses that offered low rent to students and people on a fixed income.

Her office premises were situated on the second floor of an older house that was recently renovated into professional suites. The first floor housed an architect, who owned the building, and a literary agent.

Maxine heard footsteps climbing the stairs to her office and, pausing from sanding a patch on the wall, she turned around to greet the visitor. Her father opened the door and peeked in.

"Dad, what are you doing here?"

He smiled and walked in, carrying a tool box. "Mom mentioned that you would be painting and renovating today. She also let slip that you might have need of a carpenter." He put the box on the floor and approached her to hug her. "I'm here to help with the renovations. With your passion for interior design, I know you want your new offices just right."

Maxine sighed with appreciation. "I'd hug you, but I'm filthy."

Harvey looked around the room, surveying what needed doing. "Hon, you may not hug me after you see what a lousy carpenter I am."

"You've made furniture before, and your fingers are still intact. Grab a sander."

* * * *

Three weeks later, Maxine ceremoniously installed an elegant brass plate at the entrance to her new premises. She stepped back and read aloud, "Maxine Swayman and Associates." Then she buffed the plate.

Back upstairs, Maxine glanced around with admiration. She'd created so much of it herself. Harvey and she had painted the walls a pleasant and restful taupe colour. Her glance then sought the stained glass window. She had searched and found this spectacular one through recycling and salvage companies. Now her purchase adorned the wall and gave way onto the tree-lined Gloucester Street below. In a rare private moment, Maxine's bosom swelled with pride. "Mine, all mine!"

She stared at the empty spot reserved for the brown leather sofa; exorbitantly priced. She had no choice but to put it on a payment plan. A feeling of excitement filled her at its pending arrival. Its gold button accents would match the taupe-coloured walls. She took one last look around. She would have her polished and professional look for her fledgling firm.

A deliveryman came to Maxine's second floor office.

"I need you to sign for some furniture," he said with a courteous smile. Maxine approached him.

"Where are you from?" she asked confused at the logo on his blue shirt. It was not from the furniture place she'd bought the leather sofa from.

"DeBoer's, ma'am."

"I'm confused. I ordered my couch from Bassett's in Vaughan."

"I do have the right address, according to this form here."

"There's been a mistake."

"Lady, my men are double-parked downstairs with a big table, eight chairs, and two desks.

"Don't bring the furniture up just yet.

He pushed the form at her. "Please sign here."

"I'll phone your boss and straighten out this mess."

"Her name is Jasmine and here's her number."

Maxine called the store and Jasmine came quickly to the phone. "My name is Maxine Swayman. Your deliveryman is here, claiming there's a grand delivery for me. I haven't ordered furniture from your store."

"Ms. Swayman, your lovely mother came in and

chose all of the gorgeous office furniture for you. I've never met a more generous woman." Jasmine's upbeat and cultured voice gushed while Maxine felt her face flush. "Your mother paid for everything in full. She wanted to surprise you, I guess. She was beaming with pride when she made the arrangements."

"And a surprise it is. Thank you for your time, Jasmine." Maxine returned to the deliveryman and reached for the clipboard. "The furniture's a gift! Do bring up the lot, sir." She signed hastily and went to the window to get a glimpse at her present.

It took the three professional deliverymen ninety minutes to bring up the furniture and assemble it.

They carefully placed the mahogany table where she indicated, in the reserved room for her boardroom. Eight brown leather chairs with gold buttons followed in. She could almost leap with joy.

This'll match my couch.

Next, they brought an antique advocate's desk which she had set up in her office. While they assembled the last item – a desk for her future secretary – she rummaged through her purse looking for her cheque book to give them a generous tip.

She handed each man a cheque for fifty dollars once they had terminated the job. The men left with smiles of their faces.

She hurried to her office and sat at her new desk. She ran her fingertips over its smooth surface and inhaled its wood fragrance. Already planning where she would put her supplies, she reverently opened the top drawer. A envelope came into view, and Maxine caught her name on the front of it. She picked it up and opened it. She gasped at a wad of twenty-dollar bills tied together with an elastic band. A note was at the top of the bills. She pulled it out and read, "Knock them dead, kid. Love Mom and Dad."

Maxine felt a lone tear stream down her face. *I've really made it. Mom and Dad are proud of me.*

In some small way, she resented her parents'

intrusion, but was also glad that her firm would look inviting on its very first day of business. The doorbell rang. She hurried to the top of the stairs, hoping it was the delivery people from Bassett's with the sofa.

The door opened before she got there and let out a gasp of delight at the sight of Lillian, a co-worker from her days at Stern, Perlman, Heifetz, and Zukerman. "What are you doing here?" she asked, confused but happy at the visit.

"I'd like to see the place, if it's a good time."

"It's a great time, come on in." She motioned for Lillian to come in. "I expected a sofa to be delivered."

Maxine gave her co-worker a tour then they settled into the office with freshly brewed Columbian coffee and cookies.

In between sips, Lillian asked, "Who are you considering for the secretarial position?"

Maxine shrugged. "I'll be running a newspaper advertisement. Honestly, with the decorating and negotiating of the lease, I haven't thought that far ahead."

Lillian sighed. "I'll be honest with you; the last six months at the office have bored me to death." She sighed again, louder. "I used to love my job and, don't get me wrong, I still like the people, but it's not what I want to spend the rest of my career on."

"How long have you been in family law?"

"Three years, six years in the criminal division and before that I was in corporate for six."

"You've become a fixture over there."

Lillian's gaze settled directly at her. "I want to work for you if you'll have me."

"Really?" Maxine didn't expect such a direct approach.

"Really. You and I have always gotten along. I'd like to be a part to help you build this firm from the ground up."

Now utterly uncomfortable because there wasn't any hope that she could match what Lillian was earning at the firm, she started, "Lillian," then hesitated.

"Yes?"

"I know roughly what you are making at the firm and I can't even begin to match it."

Perhaps sensing there was a possibility, Lillian quickly added, "Think about it and come up with something fair." She smiled brightly at Maxine. "I've budgeted well over the years, so as long as it's a wage I could live on, I'd jump ship to work for you."

Maxine shook her head in amazement. "I'll think on it."

Lillian asked questions about the prospective clientele. How Maxine would promote her new firm to get clients. How she would setup the reception area. Time quickly passed. Lillian finished her coffee and rose to leave. Maxine delayed her departure with a hold-on-a-minute sign. She wrote down a figure on a scrapped piece of paper and pushed it toward Lillian.

Lillian flipped the note around, scanned the figure then glanced up at Maxine. "Will you provide medical and dental coverage?"

"Of course."

"Then I'm your gal," Lillian beamed.

Maxine came around the desk and hugged her new secretary.

After settling back into her advocate chair, Maxine cleared up a nagging matter to her. "I'd like to call you an office manager and not a secretary. You have a strong skill set and the diplomacy to work with people."

Lillian's pleased look turned into a blush.

"I'm so thrilled that you stopped by."

"And me too. Now I have to go back to the office and give my notice."

"Before you go." Maxine pulled a pad. "Let's formalize it. I'll draw up an employment contract. I need you to feel secure in your decision."

"I will be even without a contract."

Maxine smiled at the confidence Lillian was showing her. "Why don't you stop by tomorrow and I'll have the contract for you. You can talk to your manager after that."

"It's a deal."

* * * *

Once she officially opened for business, Maxine became even more of a workaholic and obliged her clients in every way she could. A portion of her clientele came from the legal aid services where the Government provided lawyers for those who could not afford representation. She also had self-paying clients who paid a greater hourly rate; so as a result, she earned enough money to keep her business afloat.

Her practice developed and expanded. Maxine had the freedom, unlike in her days at Stern, Perlman, Heifetz, and Zukerman, to develop her own persona, somewhat to her surprise and her father's gratification, as a formidable and intimidating opponent that soon earned her the nickname 'Barracuda'.

Chapter Five

Kaitlyn completed her seventh year of university at the renowned University of Toronto where she received an undergraduate degree in political sciences and English.

She truly enjoyed the challenges from the university classes she took. The student lifestyle excited her. She fraternized with a bevy of students at the Hart House, but fraternity parties were too wild for her liking; people drank to excess. She avoided those shindigs.

Kaitlyn was at her happiest when she was debating politics or law with her fellow law students at an eclectic off-campus pub.

Because the drive home to Wanitou was a four-hour drive, she didn't get to visit her family as often as she wanted to, but when she did, she always sought her special cave. It held such special memories, remaining her getaway place during her entire youth.

What she remembered as a grand cavernous space, she now saw as only a moss-covered hollow in the salmon coloured granite of the Canadian Shield.

To keep at bay the boredom on campus, Kaitlyn involved herself in track and field throughout her undergraduate degree, but found that she lacked the time to commit to teams while she was in law school. She continued running as a hobby. It helped her to clear her head after a gruelling day at law school. She generally ran alone, but occasionally Anje, a fellow law student of Scandinavian descent, ran along with her.

One such a day during a jog, Anje asked, "Did you notice the tall blond man I was working out with the last time you were at the gym?"

Noting the mischevious glint in Anje's eye, Kaitlyn quickly nodded. "Did I? He's gorgeous! Are you seeing him?"

A broad smile appeared on Anje's face. "I believe it immoral, if not actually illegal, to date your first cousin – so, the answer is no."

They burst out laughing without breaking stride.

Kaitlyn knew that Anje likely had a purpose and, no longer able to contain her curiosity, she prodded, "Why do you ask?"

"He noticed you and asked me all about you." Anje gave her the look – the knowing gaze between women that said, 'what did you do to my cousin, girl?'

"You're kidding!" Kaitlyn broke stride. "Oh, my God!"

"He's definitely interested. Like me to set you up?"

Kaitlyn slowed to a fast walk. "Are you nuts?" She heaved a breath. "Between school and practically camping out at the law library, I have no time. Besides which, I have never, ever been out on a blind date, or set up, as you so elegantly call it."

Pulling her to a complete stop, Anje shook her head helplessly at her. "We don't have to do it that way. A little romance will soften that hyper-serious streak of yours. Why don't we set up something casual?"

Kaitlyn narrowed her gaze at Anje in suspicion. "Like what?"

"Why don't we all meet for a run then visit the pub afterwards?"

Kaitlyn chewed at her lips while she considered the proposition. She made up her mind and heaved a deep breath. "Guess so."

Out of habit, they resumed their run. Anje promised to call Kaitlyn after talking to Sven.

Kaitlyn followed her jog with a shower then went back to the library for an evening of studying. The courses were brutal in the third year, and Tax Law was particularly burdensome to her. She concentrated on the text book for about ninety minutes until her eyes began to lose their focus. She pushed her chair back, took a bit of a stretch, and sought the fresh air outside.

She held mixed feelings about meeting Sven. She had dated a man for six months in her first year of university. He was far less dedicated in his pursuit of a degree and resented the time she spent studying. Kaitlyn had then the all-consuming goal of getting into law school, so the relationship faded when he realized that she would never be the relaxed, free spirit he was.

Kaitlyn didn't bother with dates after that. The men in her law school were far too competitive for her tastes. The university provided many programs, and had she wanted, she could have met someone in another faculty, but she just didn't make the time.

She knew nothing of this Sven character. Was he a student or was he a career man? From her last quick perusal, she knew him to be tall, at least six feet, with finely chiselled facial features and blue eyes the colour of the sky on a bright summer day. She sighed. His short blond hair was kept in a stylish fashion. He definitely had an athletic and trim body. But the disquieting thought that he could have been a poster-boy for the Nordic race surfaced.

Despite her mixed feelings about meeting him, she was excited, hoping that he would say yes to meeting under her conditions. He was such a looker.

Remembering her studies, she returned inside the library and buried herself yet again in her tax course until ten that evening.

Kaitlyn kept to the same routine the whole next week, until all those tiny numbers turned themselves into rivers of drivel. It was time to quit.

Keeping to her disciplined self, Kaitlyn adhered to a regular training schedule, running on Mondays, Wednesdays, and Fridays. A strong mind in a strong body, she'd once remarked to Anje. Weekends were spent studying, and twice a term, she would take a weekend off to drive home and see her family. Each visit was cherished, as they were limited to six-week intervals.

A week later Anje called. Sven would meet them the following Monday at the gym. Kaitlyn agreed to go, but suggested getting a bite to eat at a restaurant instead of a pub. She was a tad uncomfortable at the idea of a first encounter in a pub. Anje agreed, understanding her predicament. They arranged a time and place for the 'date'.

Kaitlyn went for an extra run on the Saturday before the meeting. Taking her running seriously, she wanted a real workout. She had to meet with a group of law students later in the afternoon, but still had some time for herself. She ran eight laps on the indoor tract near Hart House, the equivalent of 3.2 kilometres.

After the run, Kaitlyn found herself window-shopping, something she seldom did. She spent a couple of hours browsing through Eaton's, Simpson's, and The Bay, looking for a special blouse to wear. The high prices disgusted her, until she found a cowl-neck sweater the colour of a sapphire on a clearance rack.

An education program sponsored by the First Nations community assured Kaitlyn's education. It also included a small stipend to meet her basic needs for housing and food, but treats like new clothes were exactly that, a treat. With the curriculum so heavy, she could no longer work during the school year, but had spent four summers working for the town as a lifeguard back home. It was a well-paying job for a student and she budgeted well, but she always begrudged spending money on herself. Much heavy thought went into each new purchase.

Kaitlyn amazed herself and bought the sweater. Walking back to the university along Bloor Street, she spied an unusual number of stretch limos, their occupants seemingly on sundry errands. Were they taking important people around town? Toronto had become a major movie-making centre. Which of the limousines was carrying a celebrity? Other limos, sinister ones with tinted windows, might be for mob bosses .... She shuddered at the thought, hoping to never have to defend one of those sinister persons.

She mentally shook herself back to reality and hurried back to meet her group.

* * * *

Monday arrived, and after her classes, she entered the gym to meet the others. She checked out the running track and saw no Anje or Sven. She was the first to arrive. She retired to the women's locker room and donned her shorts, a tank top, and her running shoes. She had spent a good deal more on those shoes than the sweater, rationalizing then that they were a necessity.

She was still stretching when Anje met up with her with the tall and striking Sven in tow. He spied her immediately, their glances meeting, which triggered a deep shiver within her. His eyes were the bluest that she had ever seen.

Following quick introductions, the group did stretching exercises. While they warmed up their muscles, Sven explained that he held a membership with the downtown YMCA, but at times sought out Anje here at the U of T to ensure that she kept up with her running. Anje laughed at this mention, claiming that it was she who had to drag him away from the hotel to take time-off for a jog.

Kaitlyn liked Sven immediately. She was impressed by the mutual respect the cousins shared, even through banter, and that made her at ease.

The trio began their run. Kaitlyn assessed Sven further. Nylon running shorts, a navy tank top, and scuffed Nike running shoes indicated to her that he was a hardcore runner. "Do you run often?" she asked, initiating more conversation.

"Not often enough," he confessed. "My goal is to

maintain a two kilometre run, at least three times a week, and an hour of weight training."

"That seems like plenty." Kaitlyn admired his attention to maintain a fit body.

"I really like to run, especially outside along the green space on Lakeshore Boulevard where I can see Lake Ontario."

Anje surreptitiously stabbed her with an elbow and Kaitlyn felt a smile grow on her face.

"I usualy run during mid-day so that I can also watch the young families spending time together."

As if on purpose, Anje slipped behind them, having slowed her pace. Sven and she looked over their shoulders to assess if they should also slow their pace but Anje waved them on ahead.

What a faker, she's a better runner than I am. Kaitlyn gave her a smile to say that she understood her tactic.

Sven slowed his pace but still kept ahead of Anje. "Anyway, they make these really great strollers for babies where the parent can jog behind at their pace." Kaitlyn felt his gaze bear down on her. "Last Thursday, I saw the cutest sight. A couple, about age thirty, where each of them had one of those strollers. They were jogging along with their twins. The boys took turns at dropping a toy to have a parent stop and pick it up." Kaitlyn agreed that it must have been a hilarious sight.

The trio rounded their third lap and her heart began to pound rhythmically.

Sven went on about the babies. "I slowed down my run and kept about fifty feet behind them."

"Like a stalker?" Kaitlyn teased.

"No, like a guy annoyed that he hadn't brought his video camera."

Anje's comments reached them from close behind. "That's my cousin – out to make a fast buck."

Kaitlyn turned to Sven in understanding. "I get it! You would have submitted the video to that American TV show who awards prizes for funny videos."

"You got that right!"

The three jogged for another three laps, and when they passed their starting point, Anje announced through a puffing voice, "Enough for me. You two finish your goal." Anje grabbed her towel from the stands and headed to the weight room.

Sven carried on so Kaitlyn remained with him. "But seriously, Kaitlyn, I love the outdoors, and the trail on Lakeshore is well maintained. The grass is kept free of pet excrements and garbage, and when I gaze out on the water, I hear the water lapping up on the shore. It makes a neat rhythmic sound that keeps me motivated."

"Motivated to run?"

"Well, motivated to stay in shape. The running reduces my stress levels."

She gazed at him, trying to establish what he meant by stress. "Does it help?"

"I'm a firm believer in the whole healthy body, healthy mind philosophy. I work the afternoon shift at the Opal Hotel. I have to be alert to perform my job. The best way I figured out to do this was to keep fit."

Kaitlyn deduced as much for herself. "Makes sense."

The conversation carried on while the run continued. None of those uncomfortable gaps that so often plague a first date tripped their encounter. In the process, she had extended the length of her usual run. This wasn't shabby at all.

Reaching the point where their towels were once more, Sven slowed his pace. "Well, that was our tenth lap. I've far exceeded my goal. What about you?"

"Mine is exceeded as well."

"Let's go and see what my cousin is up to."

"Hope she didn't bail on us."

His sparkling eyes smiled appraisingly at her. "And that would be a shame."

They found Anje working on an upper body contraption. Sven and she did a few strengthening exercises in the weight section, and by then, Anje was ready to end her session. Kaitlyn could tell by Anje walking aimlessly within the weight room. She had reached boredom.

Sven also noted Anje's aimless wandering. "Shower time?" he asked.

"We'll meet you in the lobby." Both girls echoed each other.

Once in the women's shower, Anje remarked, "You seem to be getting along well with Sven," over the hiss of the water.

Kaitlyn stopped lathering her hair. "He has the greatest eyes I've ever seen." Then she sighed aloud.

"Sven really likes your looks as well. He's told me that you look like a serious Pocahontas."

Kaitlyn froze. "It was going well until I got compared to a legend! How can I compete?" But she kept the disapointment from showing and resumed her shower.

They met Sven outside the locker rooms and debated where they should get a bite to eat.

"I love going to the Danforth, but you already know that, Sven," Anje remarked.

Sven shrugged his shoulders in doubt of her choice. "We've been there tons of times." He turned to Kaitlyn as if she might have a better idea. "What are you interested in?"

Having eaten only at the university cafeteria and ordinary lunch places, she avoided his gaze to hide her lack of experience. "I'm up for an adventure. You guys are from Toronto, I'm not, so let's have something different."

"Why don't we try an authentic middle eastern restaurant on Eglinton Avenue West?" Sven suggested.

"Good idea, cousin, let's go," Anje asserted, already licking at her lips. The group walked to Sven's white Nissan.

* * * *

Sven suggested the house appetizer that was pita bread

and a number of dips, including humus and baba ganoush.

Once the appetizer plates arrived, they dug in with gusto. "I don't want you guys to think I'm a braggart, but my baba ganoush is better than the one here."

"Why?"

"I put the egg plant on stoneware in a convection oven and let it become quite soft before I put it in my food processor. The convection oven seems to retain the integrity of the eggplant and its nutrients, and once I add the sesame butter, it melts together so well."

Kaitlyn swallowed a bite. "Mind you, I find this one delicious."

As if Sven took her words as a challenge, he said, "I'll make it for you one day, but I serve it with fresh cut vegetables, rarely with pita bread."

Anje nodded her approval. "I've had his baba ganoush and you do have to try it."

"Tell me about being a sous chef." Kaitlyn was curious as to what the actual job entailed.

He dabbed his mouth with the cloth napkin and began, "A sous chef is the supervisor of the kitchen under the direction of the Executive Chef, but in addition to supervising the afternoon shift, I run the line."

Kaitlyn narrowed her eyes in question.

"I should explain. The main restaurant seats one hundred and four people, and during the dinner service it fills up. Between about five and eight in the evening, it's my responsibility to ensure that meals get to the tables piping hot, and that the garnishes are top notch."

Sven's facial expression during his explanation was filled with pride, and Kaitlyn admired someone who loved his work.

"We cater to celebrities, tycoons, and people out for a special occasion. Everyone who sits at one of the Opal tables deserves the best food and the best service in the city, and I aim to please.

"When I say, run the line, I mean I shout the orders to the six cooks, some trainees, behind a long bank of stoves and ovens. Some cooks have twenty years of experience, and on the odd shift I get a lazy one who tries to act busy. Those types don't usually stay long though."

"Sounds interesting." But Kaitlyn was also fascinated by his bright white teeth as his smile widened.

"Tell me about law school," he asked her, turning the conversation around to her.

Anje stepped into the conversation. "For someone like me, it can be hell." She joked. "But a natural brain like Kaitlyn seems to sail through everything."

Kaitlyn shook her head at the way Anje belittled herself. "Anje, you do well."

"I only do well because I'm in your study group," Anje confessed. "Your bright brain rubs off on me, and I try harder because of it. If I hadn't joined your study group, I'd probably be failing."

"Hush, cousin. You've always been a straight 'A' student."

"All that changed when I got accepted to law school."

"Why?"

"I'm good at the mock court because I'm assertive, but what I find difficult is all of the memorizing of cases and case law. It's daunting."

"I feel the same way, Anje, that's why I run three times a week, to clear my clogged brain."

Anje's eyes widened. "I thought it was just me."

"It's all of us; well, maybe not Tabitha. Her nanny reads her case law as Tabitha prepares each day."

"Rrrrr!" Anje retorted, scratching the air like a cat's claw.

"Who is this Tabitha?" Sven asked between his laughter at their joke.

"Her dad is an oil tycoon in Alberta. She was educated in boarding schools all over Europe. They even spent a year in Saudi Arabia."

Kaitlyn grimaced. "Let's not talk about her tonight. I'll lose my appetite."

He looked confused. "If she's so bad, why are you in the same study group?"

"Because she's the smartest person I've ever met, and she'll make a great lawyer."

"What summer job are you applying for?" Anje asked Kaitlyn in her attempt to change the subject.

"I'm trying for a spot at the Crown's Office in downtown Toronto, but they only have positions for four summer students. I'm nervous. For economic reasons, I had to return home to Wanitou for the last two summers."

"Wanitou?" he asked Kaitlyn.

"Yes, the Wanitou First Nation on Georgian Bay. That's where I'm from."

"Do tell." Sven settled in his chair as if intent on hearing the story whether Kaitlyn felt like obliging him or not.

"My home is a bungalow on a beautiful reservation in northern Ontario. I've lived in that same house all of my life until I came to Toronto for university. Just like you, Sven, I love nature." She felt herself reliving an episode.

"I used to jog along a mish-mash of a trail along Georgian Bay. I could hardly wait for the ground to firm up in early May so I could take a gentle run on the trail. Each afternoon after chores, I'd hurry to my cave and then back again in time for dinner. I always had the same destination in mind, my mystical cave. After running about one kilometre, the granite welcomed me every time at the entrance to the cave. I must have been about twelve, or so. I'd sit on a patch of sun-warmed, velvet green moss and imagined that I was Princess Stephanie of Monaco. I'd seen baby Stephanie on our black and white television, and since then I had always wondered what it would be like to be a princess."

"Now I get it," Anje said, giggling. "You established yourself as an athlete and a voracious reader as a kid. That's how you can memorize so well."

"Yeah, and my cousin here established herself as

'the best video game player' in the family." Sven slugged Anje's arm. "You should have read more."

"Listen, little cous', I always beat you at Pac Man, so who's laughing now."

"Don't embarrass me," Sven pleaded.

"If I wanted to embarrass you, I'd get you to take us to the video arcade. Then you'd see Mr. All-Thumbs Petersen with the low score."

He gave Anje a look of warning. "Do you want me to tell Kaitlyn about when you fell out of the tree?"

"Hush."

Kaitlyn interrupted, "Look, our main course is here."

Changing the subject, Sven explained that Anje's chicken tajine included saffron, a very expensive herb. His dish was a real treat: blue cheese–crusted filet mignon, under grilled Portobello mushroom cap and onion wisps. Nervously, Kaitlyn had ordered bamia, a tomato-based stew with okra, feeling that it was likely the least exotic item on the menu.

"Delicious!" Sven exclaimed after swallowing his first bite. With a narrowed gaze, he added with an air of suspicion, "Tonight, I'm an 'undercover cater cop' destined to find the good and bad in this restaurant."

Anje waved a disinterested hand in his direction. "It's all good, cousin, it's all good. Shut up and eat!"

After dinner, Sven asked Kaitlyn if he could drive Anje home first and then drop her off next. She agreed, despite being a bit nervous about the prospect of being alone with him. He would be a gentleman, but nevertheless, she worried that she might freeze up and get tongue-tied in the car.

It would have made sense to drop her off second anyway, so there really wasn't a reason to ask.

During the drive, Sven made small talk, but she knew the moment when he was leading to asking her for a date. He looked utterly uncomfortable.

"I have Mondays and Tuesdays off, if I take them. Most times, I only take Mondays off." He paused as if searching for the right words. At the next red light they encountered, he heaved a great sigh and spared her a glance. "I'm awkwardly trying to ask you if we can do this again next Monday, just the two of us."

Her heart went into a fast flutter, then her cheeks heated up. Kaitlyn stared steadily into his sparkling eyes and said, "Oh, yes, I'd love to!"

* * * *

Kaitlyn's study group was as diverse as the city's ethnic population. She and five others frequently worked together on projects like preparations for mock trials. Tabitha, the daughter of a wealthy entrepreneur, had lived in Europe, Alberta, and Toronto. Seth, son of a grain farmer from Alberta, was a hard-working, quiet fellow and the first in his family to attend university, let alone law school. Anil, a brilliant student, had lived in Toronto for seven years, but was a native of Sri Lanka and still had the accent to prove it. He worked hard to project his voice during debates, and exuded a refined gentlemanly quality toward others. Anil, in fact, was proof positive of a lawyer's necessity of being able to step outside of his personality.

There was much theatre to being a lawyer. Joan, the eldest of the group, had worked as a social worker for nine years in the courts and had met quite a few lawyers who, she felt, were not as smart or organized as she, so she'd decided to become one. Anje rounded out the group. Anje had befriended Kaitlyn on their first day of law school. She lived in East Toronto with her mother, a doctor of family medicine, and her two sisters.

On this occasion, the group worked until six in the evening, when they called it quits. Anje, Tabitha and Kaitlyn sought dinner at a restaurant that offered wonderful giant salads at reasonable prices. The young women were escorted to a table by the window.

The waiter arrived to take their orders. Tabitha spoke up first. "I'll have a greek salad, dressing on the side, no olives, and very little red onion. Also, I'll only have the feta cheese if it's low fat."

Anje and Kaitlyn suppressed their laughter while both ordered Caesar salad with chicken strips.

"What was so funny?" Tabitha asked the moment the waiter left.

"Tab, you may as well have gotten a garden salad. You're having the kitchen remove all the good stuff."

"I have a party to go to and I'm certainly not going to smell like olives." She sighed and grimaced. "Maybe you guys have a point."

Their orders soon arrived and the women dug into their plates with appetite.

"Kaitlyn went on a date with my cousin," Anje shared with Tabitha between mouthfuls.

"Oh, really? Cool. What does he do?" Tabitha kept the chatter up.

"He's a chef at the Opal Hotel in Yorkville," replied Anje.

"A cook!" Tabitha let out, in a nasal tone.

Anje shook her head in warning. "Don't let him hear you say that or you would get an earful. A chef is someone who labours through thousands of hours of training both at a culinary school and under the apprenticeship of an Executive Chef."

"More importantly, is he a hottie?" Tabitha pressed Kaitlyn.

Kaitlyn blushed. "He's, um, not hard on the eyes at all."

Tabitha nodded as if the subject were now closed. Her gaze flitted around the restaurant, eyeing any allegedly single men. "There's no good-looking men in here. Let's not eat here again."

That last bit from Tabitha seemed to close all conversation. The women quickly finished their meals. Tabitha rose from the table first with the excuse that she had to dash to a party and quickly left.

Kaitlyn stared at Tabitha's retreating back. She had not even considered including her friends. Kaitlyn shrugged. Tabitha was like that. The others had soon learned to accept her self-centered ways.

However, Tabitha had a way of attacking arguments in study groups that kept them all on their toes. Her family's background and her extensive travels had given her a few unusual worldly views.

Anje walked with Kaitlyn as far as the subway and raised the subject of Sven's employment. "Don't listen to Tabitha's denigrating views. Sven's a really nice guy with a great career. I'm so glad the two of you hit it off. I'll let him tell you all about being a chef and the years it takes."

"I am the last person that would judge someone for their profession. I admire anything well done, even a trade like garbage pick-up. I mean, you can drop junk all over the place, or make sure it's all tidy before you move on. Sven's work sounds intriguing, and I love to eat, which is the real reason I am so dedicated to running."

"Yeah, right. I've never seen you eat all that much."

"I don't. I just eat frequently," Kaitlyn revealed with laughter as they reached the subway entrance. Following a hug, they parted ways with a simultaneous, "Let's do this again."

On Sunday, Kaitlyn allowed herself the luxury to sleep in until ten. She rose to a empty apartment, her two roommates having left already. Soon, plans for the day materialized. After a hearty breakfast of muesli, strawberry yogurt, green tea, and orange juice, she flipped on her laptop computer and worked on the course of trial procedures. Other than a trip to the grocery store for supplies, she did not leave the apartment all day.

Dinner time came along and she was still alone. She managed a meal of lasagna. After cleaning up, she called home. Her brother, still in his last year of high school, revealed his plans to attend Humber College for a law enforcement course the very next year. He claimed to take grade thirteen courses so as not to limit his opportunities. Nathan was also a runner, more of a sprinter, and he went on to apprise her of the good many competitions he'd won since her last visit.

Her mom shyly mentioned Josh Rice. The two had started dating two years previously. His wife, Janet, had died of complications from diabetes when Kaitlyn had first gone away to school. Her mom went on to tell her all about an outing she had enjoyed on Josh's boat. A picnic lunch had lead the way to some successful down-rig fishing.

Those weekend telephone calls were Kaitlyn's anchor, as on occasion a bout of homesickness would surface, especially when she she was struggling with a tough course.

Chapter Six

The insistent low hum of Kaitlyn's security buzzer in her apartment rang on Monday evening. She rushed to it and breathlessly inquired, "Yes?"

"Is Kaitlyn there?" She recognized Sven's voice.

Not wanting to appear too eager, she calmed herself and voiced, "Hi, Sven! It's me. I'll come down."

"Okey, dokey, but don't you want to know who I am?" Sven cautioned.

"Uh, yes." A nervous laugh welled up in her throat. "Who may I ask is calling?"

"Sven Petersen."

"I'm on my way." Enthusiasm sprang from her voice.

Once outside, he held the passenger door of his Nissan for her. "You look gorgeous." His tone revealed an admiration, and Kaitlyn was glad that she'd worked so hard on selecting her outfit – a teal velvet sweater and lengthy denim skirt. "I have an Italian place in mind for dinner, but first, I want to make sure it's fine with you."

"Anything will be fine." She quickly settled in and donned her seat belt.

He negotiated the streets of Toronto with ease and soon drove into the parking lot of A Taste of Venice in a section of town affectionately referred to 'Little Italy'.

"Look at the colourful street signs," she said,

pointing at them as they exited the car.

"Those are the colours of the Italian flag, didn't you know?"

"If I'd thought about it, I would have come to that realization." She smiled up at Sven. *He's so easy to talk to.* "The signs are quaint."

"Wait until you get into the restaurant." He followed his warning with a wink.

The pungent aromas of fresh baked bread and garlic aroused Kaitlyn's senses as she entered the dining room. The tables were covered in red and white checkered table clothes, with white candles as centerpieces.

"Now I know why it is so warm in here, look." She motioned to a stone fireplace.

"Rumour has it, the original owner used the very same fireplace to heat the place." They settled at a table away from the fireplace. "Today, it's just a pleasing feature to take the chill off."

They ordered Cappuccinos and perused the menus. Kaitlyn asked, "How did you get involved in cooking?"

He smiled. "I'm one of four boys and mom was so busy with work and driving us around to all our activities that I either had to learn how to cook or starve. I wasn't sure what kind of career I should go into, so I decided to try cooking first. As soon as I finished high school, I took a job in the kitchen of a roadhouse.

"I got a kick out of watching the line cooks prep the meals, enjoyed the camaraderie amongst the staff, and was just awed at the enormity of the task of cooking. What I did was fun." Keeping eye contact with her, he went on, "I had been on salads for most of summer when a line cook called in sick. The chef asked me to try working on the line and that night, although I was nervous as hell, I produced. Chef promoted me the next week and told me about an apprenticeship."

"An apprenticeship? To learn how to cook?"

He nodded gravely. "Oh, yeah. It's an intense

combination of practical learning and two years of schooling followed by a provincial exam." He flipped a page on the menu. "We should figure out what we're having for dinner before I bore you to death."

"I am hungry, but I'm also interested in learning more of your profession."

He gave her a fond smile. "Would you think it's rude if I suggested a dish or two? I love this restaurant and, if I remember correctly, you prefer healthy entrées."

"It would be cool, go ahead."

"Let's start with an antipasto appetizer. It's a platter for sharing. All the meats are thinly sliced and include prosciutto, mild salami, pancetta, and cappicola. I think you'll like the roast red peppers and giardiniera, pickled vegetables. We could follow the appetizer with a Caesar salad, and for the main course, I'd suggest eggplant Parmesan for you."

"Sounds delightful." Both of them closed their menus and placed them where the waiter could easily pick them up. "Tell me more about your training. It's a fascinating subject." Just then, the waiter arrived and took their order.

He hadn't suggested wine or a cocktail, which saved her from declining the alcohol. It pleased her.

"After my first term at George Brown College, I applied for a position at the Opal Hotel and was accepted." He sipped his Cappuccino then rested the cup on the table, his grasp remaining firm around it. "I felt bad for leaving the roadhouse where I got my first break, but I yearned for the professionalism of an upscale restaurant. I nearly quit the place on the second day."

"Why?"

"I was put on the task of shucking oysters for seven hours each day. I hated it. My hands were cold, and I kept pricking and cutting my fingers."

"What got you through the first week then?"

He looked beyond her as if recalling the event. "On the third morning, one of the first cooks invited me to sit with him at coffee break. I'll never forget it. The twenty-ish-year-old fellow revealed, 'the Sous Chef *is* testing you.' I must have looked dumfounded because he went on to explain. 'Sous Chef wants to ensure that the kids fresh out of the college are dedicated, so he gives them crappy jobs for the first two weeks to size them up.'"

Sven shook his head. "From that day on, I did whatever I was told and I've been there ever since. Enough about me, tell me about Kaitlyn Wolfe."

She shrugged. "There's not much to tell."

"I doubt that."

"I was a bookish kid who loved to read but, like you, I wasn't sure what I wanted to do when I grew up other than I liked competing in speech contests.

"Anyway, in grade ten we had a law course which enabled us to attend a court case. From the back of the courtroom I got to watch a trial. I became hooked and learned everything I could about law thereafter. I worked really hard, and my band sent me to university." Kaitlyn kept to herself her personal experience with court.

He gave a questioning look.

"I'm not referring to a rock band," she teased. "I'm a member of the Wanitou First Nation, remember? The Chief and Council of Elders administer an education fund which gives an opportunity for aboriginal kids to get an education. There's lots of poverty where I come from."

Don't tell him too much. Kaitlyn didn't know his personality well enough to venture revealing too much of herself. Rejection was difficult to swallow.

"I've heard it's nearly impossible to get into law school, how could you manage that?"

"It isn't easy," she confessed. "You must write an entrance exam and, depending on how well you score, along with your undergraduate marks, you get in." Sven nodded in understanding.

Kaitlyn caught sight of the waiter approaching them with two plates. "Here's our antipasto. Let's eat."

* * * *

The date had gone well, the conversation flowing so easily between them that it became a routine. Each Monday for the next two months, Sven courted Kaitlyn.

On the next Monday evening, they decided to go to a bookstore in downtown Toronto. He selected a book titled: *The Apprenticeship of Duddy Kravitz* by Mordecai Richler.

"That's an old book," Kaitlyn marvelled.

"I know. I read it in grade ten and just loved it. I want my very own copy."

She steered him toward the mystery and suspense section where she selected a mystery novel.

"Want to just go to a coffee shop and read?" she asked with a mischievous glint in her eye.

"Sure."

They spent the following hour reading, relaxing while sipping coffee.

"Are you okay with how our relationship is going, Sven?"

"Absolutely. Why?" A worried look spread on his face.

How was she going to tell him of her priorities? She rubbed her face and felt herself become increasingly warm. Sven was anxiously waiting for an explanation. As seconds ticked by, his worried expression became alarmed. Finally, she pulled herself together. "Sven, all I can really commit to is one evening a week. I'm not a party girl and, at twenty-six, I hope you're not missing out on fun by being with me."

He shed his worried look. One of shock replaced the latter as if she were being ludicrous. "I'm not missing out on anything! I want to be with you." His sapphire eyes shimmered with emotion. "I've never been happier than in the last couple of months. I just worry that a brain like you will bore of me."

It was her turn to be utterly shocked. "Never!"

"Me either."

With the air cleared, they relaxed and enjoyed the rest of their date.

In their new relaxed state, they dated for the remainder of Kaitlyn's second year of law school.

She still did well at school, but received her very first mark below seventy percent – a sixty-eight – in the dreaded tax class, despite all the effort she put into it. She just could not warm up to the subject; the numbers lacked humanity.

The first Tuesday of the following December, the phone rang in the evening. She reached for it. "Hi, Mom!" she greeted, hearing her mom's voice. "This is a surprise …. How come you're calling during the week? Sunday is our usual day."

"I've news that couldn't wait," Margaret replied in a harried, happy tone.

A jolt of tension coursed around the back of Kaitlyn's head. Despite her mom's bubbly tone she barely held herself together. "Concerning?"

Margaret paused as if she were searching for the right words, then she ploughed ahead all in one breath. "Nathan has just been accepted into the University of Ottawa on a partial track and field scholarship. The letter of acceptance came today."

"How totally cool! You must be so proud."

"It says the scholarship is in the amount of $18,000, and it comes with a spot on the track and field team. Nathan can also work in their university recreation department as well."

"Good for him! What's he going to take?" Kaitlyn then heard shuffling noise in the background. "Is that Nathan with you?"

"Yes. I'll let him tell you himself. Here he is."

The phone went through the usual rustlings and clunkings from being passed around, then Nathan's voice came on with the depth and resonance of a C.B.C. announcer. Little Nathan! My God, who would have thought?

"Hey, little brother, congratulations!"

"Thanks. Pretty cool, eh?"

"Very cool. So, what are you going to take?"

"Well," he paused, "remember when you kept working on me about expanding my horizons? Achieving the best I could?"

"Yeah." She waited as Nathan stretched the silence. "Yeah ... yeah," she coaxed him.

"I've been accepted into the criminology program. Once I have completed that, I'll either undertake police sciences at college or apply directly to the OPP"

"Just like Dad." She sighed, full of pride.

* * * *

During her second year of law school, all of the candidates had to secure a placement for their upcoming year of articling. Kaitlyn only knew of six other candidates who wanted to become Crown Attorneys. Everyone else wanted criminal law, civil litigation, or family law.

The competition for employment would be fierce, and one could sense the yearning for choice spots at the more lucrative offices. After all the hard work and study, a sense of entitlement filled the hearts of Kaitlyn's classmates.

For an articling position, the Crown's Office in downtown Toronto posted that they would interview only fourteen third-year law students from the entire province of Ontario. Kaitlyn's appointment was in February.

February quickly came. She thought her interview had gone rather well, but there were many other fish in the sea, and bright ones at that.

A couple of weeks later, Kaitlyn picked up a formal-looking letter from her mailbox. She opened it on the spot to find out that she hadn't been selected.

However devastating, she had never let a situation get the better of her. She persevered, contacting all of the Crown Attorney offices from Toronto all the way up to Wanitou.

She had to find a placement.

In March, she received a call from the Crown's Office in Newmarket. They were in need of an articling law student. She was asked if she were still interested in an interview. Not only was Kaitlyn interested, but flattered as well.

They had come looking for her!

She accepted the offer for an interview, and on the appointed day, which happened to be a Monday, Sven gave her a ride to Newmarket. They drove around the area to waste away the time until the appointed hour.

From Sven's comments, he also found the surrounding city limits to be exceptionally attractive, with its few preserved green spaces and even a few working farms.

Heading toward the Newmarket city building, Kaitlyn admired the numerous housing developments which were well-spaced and affluent looking, likely with price tags to match. The main street held onto its old-fashioned charm, but in the interests of modernity, hosted a shopping plaza. Newmarket reminded Kaitlyn of the town where the speech contests were held.

Their court was a regional court. With the deluge of new housing developments in the area, the population had greatly expanded and, unfortunately, so had the crime rate Kaitlyn surmised by the comings and goings of individuals. Many were members of the court and, by the subdued and upset looks of others, criminals.

Signs efficiently indicated the way to The Crown's Office, which they followed.

"If I get this job, I'll have to move to Newmarket for the summer," she whispered to Sven.

He squeezed her hand. "Enjoy the interview. If you have to relocate, then you'll have just have to. It's not a biggie."

She tugged at his hand. "I'll be further away from you."

He smiled. "Yeah, but not as far as Wanitou. Right?"

"Right." The thought cheered her up some.

Once at the door she felt a velvet kiss on her cheek. "Call me on my cell when you're done." He released her hand and patted her shoulder. "Go. While you're in there, I'll check out the local cows for mad cow disease."

She smiled at his way of lightening the mood, and as she was about to close the door, he whispered, "Love ya. Good luck."

She nodded, quietly closing the door on his retreating form.

She held her head high and squared her shoulders. Her hands were moist and beginning to shake. She flexed her fingers, not wanting to appear nervous.

As she walked by a mirrored wall, she glanced at herself, checking her appearance one last time. Having coiffed her long hair into a neat bun pleased her. With the minimal make-up she wore, she looked like a true professional, not like a student.

She was meeting with the Senior Crown Attorney, Terry Ouellette. A receptionist showed her into a conference room where a woman and a man both rose at her entrance.

Brenda Stemple introduced herself. She reached out to shake her hand and explained that she held the post of Case Administration Officer and that she would sit in on the interview.

The man followed suit. He was the Supervising Crown Attorney, Terry Ouellette. He sported a fringe of red-brown hair near the nape of his neck, but otherwise he was bald as a cue ball, with a curved, beak-like nose. The combination made him look like a wise owl.

Brenda, a trim and athletic person, neatly filled a floral print dress – she could have been a beauty contestant. The lady had matured nicely, and her skin had a light of patina.

"Why would you want to work in Newmarket?" Terry began rather abruptly as he motioned her to a seat. His voice resonated throughout the room with both volume and texture of one who had logged many hours in the courtroom. He definitely commanded a presence that compensated for his unusual looks.

Kaitlyn sat down. "I am drawn to the Crown Attorney's office, sir. It's the kind of law that I feel makes a difference in this world. Your office prosecutes the accused and helps to maintain order in society." Kaitlyn bit the inside of her cheek at the realization that her response might have sounded stiff and text-bookish. She pulled herself together and tried again.

"People carry on in the most outrageous ways and manage to weasel out of the repercussions. I want a role in preventing that from happening. You asked me why Newmarket." She paused then waved at the scene outside the window.

Drivers were looking for a space in a full parking lot and in the busy streets beyond. "It's one of the fastest growing communities in Ontario. With growth comes the criminal element. Your city appeals to me because it is renowned for its professionalism, like Toronto. In such an expanding office, I hope to provide valuable work."

Terry assessed her with a narrowed gaze. "Let me ask you this, did you try for the Crown's program in Toronto?" Kaitlyn felt her face flush, knowing full well it was his intent to assess her honesty. "Yes, sir. I was unsuccessful."

His expression softened as if she'd passed his test. "Not to worry. Toronto only has a few spots, and over the years, I've heard they are overrated. The Senior Crown Attorney tends to hire the sons and daughters of his colleagues for the choice spots. The court workers know full well that most posts are nepotism appointments. Nevertheless, we hope to hire a couple of pseudo-interns for the summer."

She paused briefly. Her curiosity winning over, she asked, "What is a pseudo-intern?"

"Newmarket doesn't have a well-padded budget like Toronto, but I managed to divert funds from my administrative budget and, although most of your tasks would be clerical in nature, you would gain courtroom experience."

A knot formed in her stomach. She was a bright law student with an 'A' average. She shouldn't have to perform clerical duties while her fellow students got law experience.

Brenda Stemple, who had been quietly doodling on a legal pad, spoke up, "The successful candidate will assist me in setting up victim interviews, interfacing with the Victim Witness Support Professionals, and will also assist Terry in court." An excitement filled her chest while Brenda explained in more details.

"You would sit in on interviews where victims of family violence learn, probably for the first time in their lives, that they have rights and they no longer have to endure a life of abuse. You would hand-hold older ladies whose rent cheques were stolen by their own grandsons. You will participate in the nitty-gritty of this office. The value of what we do is, I think, beyond calculation." Brenda, in contrast with Terry, smiled reassuringly, exposing enormous teeth that reminded Kaitlyn absurdly of Chiclets gum.

Kaitlyn didn't miss Brenda's terminology discretely changing from 'the applicant' to 'you'. Kaitlyn then felt that she had met a kindred spirit in Brenda. For the first time in the interview, a reserved freedom to be enthusiastic invaded her mind without appearing to be too much of a 'gee-whizzer'. So many lawyers were much too serious to appreciate a 'gee-whizzer'; one had to be careful.

"Tell me your opinion of the Young Offender's Act," Terry asked brusquely, commanding her full attention.

Her mind quickly wandered to her childhood enemy, Stacey Cummings, who'd gotten off her charge of assault with a slap on the wrist. Stacey'd been convicted, and after completing her probation, she'd received a pardon. Kaitlyn caught herself before she let slip an inappropriate personal story in an interview. She searched for, and felt she quickly found, the right words.

Jacqui Morrison

"When we're young, our bodies and certainly our minds are not fully developed. Teenagers experiment and take silly risks without regard for the consequences. A student might, on a dare from friends, pour dish soap in the town fountain at Hallowe'en, or he may try marijuana and get caught. Could this same 'A' student be an asset to society when he becomes a man? I'd have to say yes. I'd have to say that the anonymity of the Young Offender's Act allows the ... youth to be punished for his foolishness, but it doesn't force him to carry a criminal record for the rest of his life. It gives him a second chance to change his ways."

Kaitlyn stopped before she eventually put her foot in her mouth, but Terry seemed to pick up that she had more to say.

"Go on."

Carefully, Kaitlyn explained further, "The Act does have its flaws. Some youth *are* dangerous, and they mock the milder consequences of the punishments under the Act. Currently, the decision-makers are working with the Attorney General to come up with a stronger and more effective Act. At the moment, a twelve-year-old can murder someone and will not be incarcerated. In my opinion, this is fundamentally wrong. Murder is an adult crime, just by its nature. In general, though, I do believe in the fact that the records are sealed so the youths can develop into adults without worrying that their future is over before it began."

Terry nodded in satisfaction. "Good answer. I like your style and convictions. Now can you to tell me the difference between summary and indictable convictions?"

He seems to approve of me, don't blow it now.

"A summary offence is a crime that is considered less serious and is given a lesser penalty. When explaining it to a client, you might call it a misdemeanour, an American term. With the prevalence of U.S. television shows on law, people tend to understand that term better. Summary cases are tried in a lower court known as the Provincial Courts by a provincial court judge. Indictable offences are considered more serious, and if convicted, lead to longer sentences."

"Good, good." Terry again nodded, showing his approval. "Now can you tell me about a hybrid case and how it relates to the crown's office?"

Kaitlyn's mind momentarily returned to her textbook on criminal law, and she envisioned the page where these cases were defined. "A hybrid, by definition, can go either way. It can be either a summary offence or an indictable offence. The Crown Attorney's office decides how to proceed on a hybrid offence."

Throughout her answers, she noticed Brenda jotting notes and smiling at her in between her scribbles. Kaitlyn's confidence grew with each question. *I even sound like a lawyer!*

An hour of questioning ended with Terry saying, "I can hire two interns this summer, and after the formality of reference checking, one of the jobs will be yours." He reached for her resume and visually sought the top partition on it. "Do I call you at the number on the top of your resume?"

"Yes," Kaitlyn confirmed.

Terry acknowledged with a curt nod and rose from his chair. Kaitlyn also rose. "You sure do." She reached out to shake his hand. "Thank you so much. I really appreciate your interest in me." With pride, she shook Terry's hand then Brenda's.

Expecting her hand to be moist from a case of the nerves, she was pleasantly surprised when her hands were dry. She left the office, head held high, with perfect posture.

Outside the courthouse, she called Sven on his cell phone and he soon drove by to pick her up.

"How'd it go, hon?"

She sat down in the passenger seat and closed her eyes. "Give me a few minutes to digest everything." She took a few deep breaths then propped one eye open in his direction. "Let's talk over lunch."

Sven smiled and drove off. Kaitlyn and he simultaneously spotted a British pub. Sven swerved into their parking lot and parked the vehicle.

They entered a room decorated with old railway and steamship travel posters. It also boasted a real red British phone booth. Their menus listed such items as cockaleeky soup and steak-and-kidney pie.

The waiter took their order and wandered off to the kitchen. Kaitlyn took a deep breath and proudly declared, "I've been bursting to tell you. They are looking strongly towards me for the summer law intern job."

"That's great, Kaitlyn! It's the first step in the door."

"It's not exactly what I wanted, but I'll get to spend some time in the criminal court if my work's done." She reached for the recently filled water glass and downed half of it. "Sorry, my throat is so parched from answering so many questions. And both persons I'll be working for seem very approachable." She smiled, now at ease and satisfied with herself. "As you said, it's the first step in the door."

"It's pretty important to like the people you work with." She agreed with him with a nod. "I won't have to commute to northern Ontario to see you." Sven beamed his good-natured smile that always melted her heart. "What are you planning to do about living accommodations?" A trace of concern had chased away his smile.

She shrugged. "I have no idea."

"You have two months. That's plenty of time. I don't think it will be too difficult to find something. We'll grab a local paper on the way out of town, okay?"

"Okay." She rubbed her hands together. "Let's eat. I like lots of different cooking, but the British stuff really fills you up."

"It's the pit-stop of cuisine."

* * * *

After her run, Kaitlyn stepped under a steamy shower and then draped her body in her soft velour housecoat. She laid across the couch, and fell into an impromptu nap.

The ringing of a telephone awakened her. On the fifth ring, she was awake enough to make sense. She answered it. A deep voiced male asked, "Kaitlyn?"

"Yes."

"It's Terry Ouellette calling. I'd like to offer you the summer intern job."

Now fully awake, heart pumping wildly, she answered, "I accept, Terry. Thank you."

"We'll offer you the wage that was posted with the call for interviews. Your start date is May 15th. You'll be done with exams by then, won't you?"

"I sure will."

A pause followed then Terry went ahead. "Brenda and I were impressed with your interview. Toronto's loss is our gain. We believe that you didn't get the intern job in Toronto because your previous summers had been spent working for the town of Harrisville instead of at a law firm."

"I couldn't afford the rent in Toronto, so I returned home to lifeguard."

"The housing prices in Toronto are insane, which is part of the reason I, myself, prefer Newmarket. It's a vibrant community. You'll enjoy working here."

"I won't disappoint you."

"Please report to Brenda's office on May 15th. She'll provide your orientation and .... Welcome aboard."

"Thank you."

* * * *

The following Saturday, Sven and Kaitlyn drove up to Newmarket and visited rental apartments. They found a one-bedroom basement apartment which felt cozy and inviting; however, Sven had to duck each time he moved between rooms. He claimed he didn't mind his discomfort if she wanted the apartment.

Kaitlyn just adored the bright yellow sunflowers painted on the livingroom walls. Since it was within walking distance to the courthouse, she wouldn't need a car right away.

The family was renting out their basement to cover their high mortgage expenses and was agreeable with holding the place until the first of May.

* * * *

The hallway at the University of Toronto law school seemed longer and foreboding this time around, a dark tunnel of questionable destiny. As Kaitlyn negotiated her way to the bulletin board, Dr. York, the taxation professor, waddled out of his office and pinned up the marks for his class then scurried away like a bearded little criminal to avoid the inevitable firestorm of protests, entreaties, and lobbying from students already waiting expectantly.

Seeking one's mark at the bulletin board was a ritual university students referred to as 'going to the wall'. The loud gurgling of her stomach, a sure sign of her nervousness, resulted in some stares, yet she harboured a steely determination, approaching the looming bulletin board. Results were posted under the students' identification numbers instead of their names, a policy to ensure privacy for all. Kaitlyn had her number memorized.

As students vacated the area of the board, either happy or disgusted, others filled in the vacant spots.

Kaitlyn reached the list.

She anxiously perused the list, looking for her student number. Under her nine digit reference number, she read her mark for the semester, sealing it into memory.

She clutched her stomach and sought the nearest

chair. Other students jostling around the bulletin board were too preoccupied to notice her tears.

Seventy-four percent. She had pulled her average up to the seventy percent mark! And, more importantly, she would never have to take taxation again. An ominous cloud lifted.

Her struggle for an adequate mark had been a very humbling experience. Everything else she had accomplished through hard work and preparation. It was unlike her to work so hard on one course. She hoped she would never have anything to do with the topic of taxation again.

* * * *

Three days after completing the university year, Kaitlyn started her summer internship term at the Newmarket courthouse. The duties turned out to be a pleasant challenge. Brenda was very efficient and a great mentor. Kaitlyn fit in well within the team and welcomed the workload, working long and tedious hours the first couple of weeks.

Kaitlyn was still at her cubicle when the sun began to set. The front door opening startled her. She peered around the cubicle wall and caught Brenda rushing into the office in a black evening dress, her make-up precisely applied.

Brenda hurried into her office, then exiting from it became aware of the light left on in the outer offices. She paused as if to decide whether she should interfere or not, then she headed straight for Kaitlyn's cubicle. "What are you doing here?" she asked, a motherly, concerned look on her face.

"I'm catching up on filing." Kaitlyn nodded at her dress. "I could ask you the same thing. You look gorgeous."

"Thanks. I'm going out on a date with my husband and I had forgotten my pumps here."

"Date? With you husband?"

Brenda shrugged, sparing her a you-know glance and, at Kaitlyn's blank look, she explained, "Every month, we go out for dinner or to the theatre." Brenda smiled, letting out a sigh of anticipation."We dress up. We have fun. It keeps our marriage alive and vibrant."

"Neat!"

"Now tell me, why are you filing so late at night?"

"Remember when you said that if I get my work done I can spend time observing in the courtroom?" Kaitlyn grinned widely. "That's why."

"Makes sense, but there's more to life than work, kiddo. Be careful."

"I will."

* * * *

On the Friday of her third week at the crown attorney's office, Kaitlyn was walking by Brenda's cubicle when she overheard her mentor speak to another party on the phone.

Hearing her name mentioned, she craned her neck to hear more. "We may have underestimated Kaitlyn."

Her curiosity fully peaked, but not willing to get caught eavesdropping, Kaitlyn paused on her way to the photocopier. "She's incisive and, this morning, when we interviewed the last sexual assault victim, she really put the client at ease while preparing her for court". A pause followed and Brenda's voice rose, ever so slightly. "Yes, Terry, you're right. Kaitlyn is the best intern we've hired so far."

She felt a smile of contentment form on her face, and photocopier forgotten, she soundlessly walked back to her own cubicle.

* * * *

The summer flew past and Terry assured her that once she was called to the bar, he would hire her as an Assistant Crown Attorney, if an opening arose. Nine other crown attorneys worked in the office, and Kaitlyn felt they would be there for years to come. Her good humour sank, but she hid it well. Nearing her last day, her co-workers took her out to dinner to thank her for the hard work she'd provided. And to round out her successful summer, she was handed a glowing letter of reference. Lastly, promises to keep in touch were mutually dispensed.

Chapter Seven

The fall of 1993 flew as if on an autumn wind. Kaitlyn released bit by bit her anxiety that had lingered after her father's death. She drew closer to Sven. For years she'd believed that, if she ever became close to a man again, she would lose him by death or by desertion. It was a foolish assumption that permeated her being for many years.

Through his light-hearted ways of dealing with life, Sven had a way of showing her a world reborn, which brought to Kaitlyn a renewed sense of security.

Sven's sunny nature and kind spirit were such restorative influences that maybe life should just carry on as is. With him, her self-confidence blossomed.

On plenty of occasions, she'd wondered if counselling would in fact help her dump some of the emotional baggage she'd carried from her childhood, but she'd chosen not to seek the help.

Following a pleasant dinner out, Sven took her to admire the Christmas sights in downtown Toronto. It was so near Christmas, and both enjoyed simple things like watching children mesmerized by a particular Christmas display in one of the store windows.

The scene before her had Kaitlyn recalling her childhood vision of standing with a tall, good-looking Nordic man. Her childhood fantasy had come true, she mentally told her mirror image in the glass.

A giddy mix of euphoria and optimism seeped into her being, and for the moment, she wanted to hold onto it forever. She turned to him. "I love you," she said impulsively, grabbing his neck.

She was ready for an embrace, but Sven recoiled, an appalled look at her action. Then his face-hardened. "Not here, Kaitlyn." He pried Kaitlyn's arm from around his neck.

The precious, joyous moment that had filled her heart seconds before now evaporated, replaced by an overwhelming ache, a deep slice from a sharpened blade.

"We'll talk at my place," Sven said, in way of explanation. Abruptly turning from the window, he walked on at a fast pace. He gave no other explanation for his sudden sullenness. She walked beside him in stunned misery and shame, unable to figure out what had precipitated such a change in mood.

Once they walked over the threshold of his apartment, the old Sven was back, pulling Kaitlyn against his chest.

"You've got to be kidding." She shoved him away without any qualms.

"What's wrong?"

Now was the perfect time to demand an answer for his cold as stone behavior out on the street. "Why in hell did you go so weird on me when I told you I loved you?"

He approached her again with an apologetic smile. "It wasn't the words, my dear. It was the show of affection."

She held up her hand to stop his advance. He froze. She shook herself mentally. Was she being castigated? She got thoroughly confused. *If he loves me, why is he being such an ass?*

The question precipitated even more caution. She looked at her lover; a man she barely knew at this very moment.

Sven began, "I love you as well, but I'm working really hard for my promotion. It's unprofessional for a

Sous Chef in an upscale restaurant to smooch on a sidewalk. If we were seen by the wrong eyes, well ...."

"Aren't you a bit paranoid? No one was around, and even if they were, you were on your own time."

Sven sighed his frustration loudly. "I didn't think you'd understand. Let me explain. Most of the Executive Chefs are Europeans who tend to marry passive doting wives. I'm with a beautiful and strong future lawyer, and that is raising eyebrows. It's a cultural thing, you see. I can't take any chances. And I, personally, don't want my private life on display, okay?"

Kaitlyn hadn't missed his condescending tone through the last sentence. "I get your point," she said, mimicking his tone. With one vicious swipe, she grabbed her purse that, seconds before, she'd dropped to the floor, and turned toward the door. "I'm heading home."

"Are you pissed off at me?"

Was he kidding? She stopped and turned around to confirm it. He seemed to be literally puzzled by her actions. "Yes! I don't appreciate your draconian code of conduct. Wake up, Sven, I'm going to be a lawyer. I'll never be the doting wife buzzing in the background."

Sven's open mouth told her he was at a loss for words. On her way out, she slammed his front door.

* * * *

Sven did come around and, in time, became less over-bearing. She still loved him. However, his European upbringing still influenced his private life as well as his professional one. But, over the winter, Sven grew to appreciate more the ways of Canadian living.

The spring of the next year proved to be quite a challenge as Kaitlyn was working on her final courses. The studies and examinations were brutal and, without the motivation of the study group, not to mention sheer self-determination, her survival in law school would have been questioned.

Recreation was sporadic. One evening, Kaitlyn, thoroughly brain-drained, was lounging at Sven's apartment. A rare treat of truly 'vegging out' in sweat pants, she was glued to the television while the show *Mad about You* was on. Until the phone rang.

"Phone, hon." Kaitlyn coaxed Sven to answer as she lay on the couch, pleasantly engrossed in the show's silliness.

Sven grumbled, reluctant to reach for the phone resting on the hall table and miss out on a second of the television series. He passed the cordless phone to her, mouthing: "It's your boss."

"Hi, Terry. How are you?"

Terry's voice was cheery. "We offer a full benefits package after three months including extended health, dental, and whatnot. Human resources will fill you in on this. Your wage as a new articling Crown Attorney will be forty percent above what you were making as an intern. There's a system that as you gain experience, your salary will rise accordingly."

Still in shock, Kaitlyn could only manage, "I see."

"Are you interested?"

She leaped off the couch. Struggling to maintain a business-like tone, she answered, "Yes, I am. When do I start?"

"Next Monday if you can. The following week if you have other commitments."

"I have finals for the next three weeks."

"How about the first Monday following your finals?"

"That would be perfect, Terry."

"Welcome aboard." Terry hung up the phone.

She laid the phone on the nearest coffee table and turned to Sven, beaming. "He's offered me the articling job and I've accepted. Now I must pull through the finals." Kaitlyn went into a jumping up and down routine like a kid.

Sven reached for her, and when he got a firm hold, they hugged jerkily.

She stopped her bouncing and drew back. "I hope you don't think I'm being childish."

"Childish, no; enthusiastic, yes." He pulled her into him once again, patting her back in his own way of congratulating her.

"I start right after finals," she said, her voice muffled as they fell into a deep embrace.

Garments flew with wild abandon and soon they were making frantic love, initially on the couch, then after slipping off of it, in a heap onto the floor. He pushed the coffee table out of their way and deeply kissed her.

"I love you," she admitted again once Sven pulled his scorching lips away.

"I love you more." He winked. "You're beautiful. I just love those coffee-hued eyes of yours." He then went on to skilfully kiss her throat with a gentleness, unlike the frenetic lovemaking of moments before.

She brushed blond strands of hair off his face, rejoicing in the feel of his warm, moist skin. He then buried his face on her breasts.

He's a beautiful man. She moaned as he pleasured her and she caressed him.

"It's your turn now to be pleasured." She winked back at him with the promise of pleasurable feelings. And the lovemaking continued for another hour.

An exhausted, perspiring, and thoroughly sated Kaitlyn shrouded herself in Sven's cotton bathrobe. After sharing a hot shower together, they moved to his bed where they slept, peacefully, in each other's arms.

* * * *

During the last three weeks of law school, Kaitlyn didn't see Sven or anyone else socially. She only worked out sporadically and could barely get enough sleep. The hard work and determination finally paid off. Kaitlyn achieved the eighth place in her graduating class of 103.

The study group and their friends organized an epic party to celebrate the completion of their formal three years of university. Following an elegant dinner at a downtown restaurant, they moved the festivities to a dance club, where they 'made merry', as a neo-Elizabethan member of the party put it, until two in the morning.

Of all her friends, Kaitlyn figured that Anje would be the only one she was likely to see throughout her articling year, but she would try to stay in touch with the others. Shared experiences would be valuable for the coming bar admissions course, in six months time following articling. More courses and examinations would follow, even more difficult than what they had just endured. The sobering possibility of failing, even in the wake of hard work in pre-law, loomed ahead.

To avert such a dreadful outcome, Kaitlyn's study group resolved to re-constitute itself when they resumed their attendance at university.

Kaitlyn rented the same apartment as she had the previous year, which was so conveniently near the courthouse. Since she would be earning more money, the time to own a car had come.

She and Sven wandered the used-car lots, hunting for a bargain – a suitable vehicle in good operating condition. She soon fell in love with a sweet red Datsun 240, for which she could manage the payments. She could now get back and forth to work faster and still have a bit of fun during her off time for a reasonably priced tank of gas.

The workload in the first week completely overwhelmed her. The material Kaitlyn had to prepare each day was, in her first few weeks, all but unmanageable. University hadn't prepared anyone for the harsh realities of Provincial Criminal Court. In law school, the study group had agonized over each argument and each mock case as though it were a real case. In criminal court, the sheer number of cases and motions remained a constant battle against time, the difference seeming like a cross-country runner pacing himself and a sprinter racing frantically to cross the finish line.

Unable to balance her workload in her inaugural

week, she chose to forgo her exercises and still ended up with little time for her personal life.

Kaitlyn spoke briefly to Sven on the Wednesday; she was sluggish, overtired, unable to carry a decent conversation. She finished the call with Sven telling her that he would try to spend most of Sunday with her.

Brenda, the court coordinator, who had become a great ally the previous summer, relieved some of Kaitlyn's pressure with her efficient manner and pleasant personality. Terry seemed busier than she remembered, but now, with her new position, she began to perceive him in a different light.

Kaitlyn learned to think on her feet very quickly. Within days, she discovered which lawyers had integrity and which did not. The rumour mill at the courthouse was more intense than anything that she had ever encountered in her university life. She would have to show strength at all costs and muster every ounce of dignity as she balanced the work between the ten Crown Attorneys.

* * * *

"Quota hiring, I'd say," Duncan Wright, an Assistant Crown Attorney, muttered to Trevor Knight, another Assistant Crown.

In the closest pub to the courthouse, Brenda and Kaitlyn were seated on the other side of the booth, hidden from view of the two men talking. Both women could not help but overhear the conversation.

"What the hell are you talking about?" Kaitlyn recognized Trevor's voice.

Duncan Wright seemed to hesitate, but only for a moment. "That native girl, Wolfe, her last name is. She must be filling some sort of minority quota program."

Not this again. Kaitlyn blushed and sighed inwardly, while slumping againt the back of her booth. The unsavoury Stacey Cummings memory returned to haunt her.

Brenda's facial expression turned from utter shock to avoidance. She remained silent. When a bottle hit the next table, both of them startled.

"Where would you get an idea like that?" Trevor said with a hint of unpleasantness in his voice. "She's smart and will make a great lawyer."

"I'll give Duncan a piece of my mind," Brenda said in a whisper and began to shuffle to the edge of the bench. Her earlier shock was now morphing into anger.

Kaitlyn shook her head, whispering back, "Leave it be, Brenda."

Duncan, unaware of the women being within earshot, went on with his theory. "Hey, I'm just saying Terry never hired an articling lawyer before and, suddenly, from the secretarial pool comes an articling Crown. Don't you find this the least bit suspicious?"

"She wasn't a secretary. Brenda Semple was swamped. Terry used administrative dollars to hire Kaitlyn last summer. She performed legal work and clerical details. Hell, Duncan, law students have to start somewhere. Brenda has told me that Kaitlyn does a terrific job interviewing rape victims. She has this natural honesty going for her, and she knows how to make victims feel safe. She's no quota hire, bud. Let's drop this subject and talk about something else."

Brenda pressured her with a don't-let-Duncan-get-away-with-this look.

Kaitlyn shook her head once more. "This is all so embarrassing. But please, Brenda, could you let this go?"

Brenda nodded, reached for Kaitlyn's hand and gave it a warm squeeze.

Within a few minutes, the men vacated their booth and left the premises without ever being conscious that Kaitlyn had been seated practically right on top of them.

The men's departure cleared the air, and conversation between Brenda and her took off.

"I've grown rather curious of you. Tell me about yourself, Kaitlyn. I mean the real you, not the articling person."

Kaitlyn smiled. "I grew up on a beautiful land called the Wanitou First Nation on the Georgian Bay shore. The village I lived in was small; everyone knew everyone else. I felt safe there. I took the school bus to town every day, along with the kids from town." She grew serious and shrugged. "I encountered racism from small-minded girls. It was dreadful at times."

"I'm sorry to hear that."

"Brenda, I don't want to sound maudlin, but in our multi-cultural country, many people have encountered racism; I'm sure my stories aren't unique."

"Probably not, but I'll learn more about the real Kaitlyn, if you want to share."

Kaitlyn felt her thoughts drift, go back in time. "I remember being in the girls' washroom three days after winning my first speech competition. Still on a high, I was out of sight, secluded in one of those gawd-awful cubicles they have in elementary schools. No one knew I was in there.

"I heard footsteps, voices. One girl I easily recognized as Stacey Cummings, a snotty privileged type. The other then became obvious, Stacey's friend, Gwen, a follower type. To this day, I remember Stacey's words, as though she'd spoken them just a few moments ago."

"Go on," Brenda prodded.

"Stacey said, 'My mom is not impressed that Brad didn't win the speech contest. She says he lost because of quotas.' Gwen went on to ask what was a quota, and in an officious and arrogant voice, Stacey explained, 'Officials must give enough treats to minorities so they won't get angry and rebel. They gave the award to Kaitlyn Wolfe to keep the Indians happy. In my opinion, Brad's speech was much better. My mother says that Kaitlyn's subject was just a dumb idea and has nothing to do with us. She thinks the judges felt pressured in awarding the award to an Indian this year, and probably next year, they'll have to give it to another minority.' "

Brenda looked stunned. "What did you do?"

"Well, as you can imagine, I was furious, but I didn't let that brat get away with her cruel words. I took that exact moment to flush the toilet. I opened the bathroom door and went to the sinks, ensuring that I looked composed. There were three sinks in the girls' bathroom and, without making eye contact, I walked up to the unsused one and washed my hands.

"I reached for the paper towel, then paused. I first caught sight of Gwen. She looked afraid and kept her glance averted, but meanwhile, Stacey had braced herself with an expression of pure malice.

"I stared both girls down then asked, 'Can quotas use this paper towel, or should I petition to get my own paper towel rack? The girls' faces went beet red. 'No, it's for everyone,' quavered Gwen. I then left the bathroom, feeling rather sad and lonely."

"What a couple of small-minded losers," Brenda commiserated."

"Stacey Cummings goaded me all throughout public school and high school. Every time I enjoyed a small success, she'd gossip and carry on as if I only succeeded because I was a minority, a total pile of horse shit."

"No doubt. That was a hard way to grow up. You've done really well for yourself. Now, I wonder what that bigoted girl would be doing these days."

"I didn't really hear much about her after high school. She's probably working at something menial." Kaitlyn giggled. "She wasn't the smartest."

Brenda patted Kaitlyn's hand. "That was then, this is now. Just ignore Duncan. He's a dork anyway. Care for nachos? They'll go well with this Sangria."

* * * *

Each morning, Kaitlyn faithfully entered the office at eight, and she rarely left before six in the evening. She started each day with a specific plan, but by lunchtime, priorities had shot her plan out of the window. By Murphy's Law, one phone call unravelled the entire day.

At breaktime that day, Brenda stopped by her cubicle with an offer. "How about we get a coffee from the park vendor, sit on park bench, and enjoy the day?"

"Sounds nice, Brenda, but I've got too much work."

Brenda sighed loudly, exasperated. "That's exactly why I want you to break and have coffee with me."

Kaitlyn gave her a curt nod of resignation. "I'll be ready in fifteen minutes." She smiled, meaning it.

"I'll come and fetch you. I don't trust you to come out on your own."

* * * *

Coffees in hand, they leisured on a park bench, with their backs to the courthouse.

"Isn't this beautiful?" Brenda asked in a convincing tone as they sat surrounded by an immaculately maintained garden. "Look at the impatiens. Their lives are so short, from late spring to the first frost."

Kaitlyn watched as the impatiences moved as one under the stress of the wind.

Brenda turned to her, her facial expression sombre. "I must apologize to you, Kaitlyn; I didn't bring you outside our building to admire and talk about flowers." Brenda took a deep breath, then went on. "I have something serious to discuss with you."

"Is anything wrong?" Kaitlyn's mood plumetted. Had she mishandled a case?

"Not with me, but I'm seriously concerned about you. I've noted that you rarely take a lunch break, or any breaks for that matter. I've begun to notice signs of fatigue in you by the afternoons. I've seen you substitute a chocolate bar or potato chips for a proper meal."

"But ...."

"It's taken me a few days to pluck my courage to talk to you about this. Let me first get my points out before you argue. My niece, Rebecca, was much like you. She wasn't a lawyer but a stockbroker." Kaitlyn caught the moisture pooling in Brenda's eyes. "At thirty-two years old, she suffered a massive coronary. Her boss found her slumped over her desk. Dead."

"That's horrible."

"My sister, Rebecca's mother, never really got over it." Brenda's tears became more pronounced. "Rebecca was driven, like you, but she never took time to smell the flowers. She never married, never had any children. Now my sister aches every day for her."

Kaitlyn put an arm around her friend's shoulder and gave her a light squeeze.

When Brenda recovered enough from her pain, Kaitlyn admitted, "I thought only men had heart attacks."

Brenda shook her head, a miserable look still on her face. "That's the sad part. Women have them just as well and for the same reasons. Stress, lack of exercise, bad eating habits, and heavy drinking are all warning signals. Until she died, we never knew that Rebecca liked her scotch on the rocks.

"You remind me of her, in certain ways. Your succeeding at a young age in a profession which used to be dominated by men." Brenda wiped away a final tear, and her voice got stronger. "Keep up this pace, young lady, and you'll become ineffective. Your co-workers will resent it if you get sick from poor nutrition and lack of sleep. You're a beautiful woman, and a dear friend. I don't want you to end up like Rebecca."

"I'll change my ways, I promise I will." She gave Brenda a final hug to seal her promise.

Brenda straightened, taking on a supervisor demeanor. "Starting tomorrow lunch, I expect you to take at least twenty minutes out of the building for a walk, shopping, or absolutely anything else but work. We can walk together if you'd like."

Kaitlyn beamed at the idea. "I'll bring my running shoes."

Brenda rose and smiled fondly at her. "I'll meet you at noon tomorrow." She looked at her watch and gasped.

"Oh dear, I have a meeting in five." She began edging backwards toward the courthouse.

"Thanks for the talk," Kaitlyn said, meaning every word and waved her off.

Knowing perfectly the need for self-care and having worked on balance throughout university, Kaitlyn berated herself. How could she have allowed the situation to deteriorate? Her all-consuming desire to succeed at all costs and her workalcolic ways had become a nefarious habit, a way of life. The important life lessons that she'd acquired early on in life had diminished in importance until Brenda's wise reminders.

Ironically, once she started to take breaks and eat healthier, Kaitlyn handled the stress and chaos far more effectively. Her anxiety level diminished, and, although she kept her will to succeed, her life was much more balanced. Sven also mentioned that he'd noticed a change for the better. Their mid-week telephone calls became much less strained.

After gruelling days at the courthouse, Kaitlyn would sometimes envision her magical cave in different seasons while she lay, waiting for sleep to claim her. From the frost-covered moss and snow-covered rocks, to the rebirth of the earth in the spring where waters would again flow toward the bay.

The sight line from the cave onto the bay had given her a clear view of swaying maple and pine trees. In the brilliance of summer, canoe-ers, kayak-ers and swimmers enjoyed the pristine water, and she who loved the warmth of the rock and moss beneath her body was revelling in mother nature's cocoon.

Her favourite season, without question, was autumn, where the deities would paint the maple leaves a brilliant cascade of yellows, oranges, and reds, and the tall pines would bend and sway under cooler gusts, like giant fishing rods.

Autumn memories and images provided her with the best respite. She would relive runs through the trails under the fall colours with the sun beating down her back, her hair flowing in the wind.

While she no longer believed in her childhood fantasies about the magic the cave withheld, its state of being provided a warm memory in her soul. The visualizing became a ritual which prepared her to fall asleep, promoting within her a sense of inner calm. Her memories also included a chubby Nathan, and how he cuddled up to her. His cute little laugh always brought on a feeling of wellness inside her. Her mom's giggles were infectious as well.

Once in a while, pleasant memories of her dad would sneak into her dreams, giving her a secure feeling. Had he lived, he would have been very proud of the adults that she and Nathan had become.

* * * *

For the first three months of her articling job, Kaitlyn did not have the energy or interest in looking for her own place yet. On weekends, if she weren't at Sven's, she would either visit Nathan at the University of Ottawa or drive up to Wanitou to see her mom.

Arriving on the Wanitou Territory in her fancy sports car always brought on stares from the youngsters. They were particularly fond of Sven.

Sven's career didn't allow him many weekends off, so it was truly a treat when he accompanied her to Wanitou. He also enjoyed the beauty of natural habitat, claiming it reminded him so much of his ancestral Nordic past.

He kept saying that he loved to visit with Margaret and Josh Rice. Sven would spend a lot of time fishing with Josh while her mom and her would sit quietly in the boat and read, occasionally participating in the netting of a fish. Those fishing occasions always followed with an enormous shore lunch. Fresh pickerel over an open fire, salads and homemade rolls were something only to be had in Ontario's north country, although Margaret once jokingly brought canned spaghetti, in case Kaitlyn's city-slicker boyfriend ruined Josh's fishing technique.

Kaitlyn journeyed to Wanitou on her own twice in the first three months of her articling position. On those weekends, she would run, never neglecting to visit her special cave. The memories were much more compelling than the reality of the cave, but it didn't matter to her. It was still her private place, where she could think, imagine, and watch the clouds scurry by while the sunshine sparkled on the waters of the Georgian Bay.

In early August, Sven took the long weekend off, and through his employer, booked a suite at the Opal Chateau located in Montreal.

Friday evening was spent driving to Montreal, checking into the hotel shortly after ten. To Kaitlyn's delight, the suite was luxurious. Finely crafted furniture, lavish draperies, and bed linens fit for royalty adorned the room. They checked out pubs in the Old Montreal while taking pleasure in the mix of tourists. Locals spoke in either French or English, the official tongues, while foreign students spoke a variety of other languages. Even though it was still summer, students were winding up their summer courses, gearing up for the fall term at McGill, Concordia, and the University of Montreal.

Saturday began at ten with room service. Sven tipped the waiter and brought Kaitlyn's tray to her in bed. On the tray, a single red rose lay beside her plate of omelette. Kaitlyn's eyes were adjusting to the glare of morning sunshine, and while enjoying the wonderful aroma of coffee and omelette, she noticed a black, velvet-covered jewellery box. "What's this?" she asked Sven, pointing to it. He smiled wickedly at her.

Sven went down on one knee and her heart went into flutters at the meaning of Sven's action.

"Kaitlyn, you are my world, will you do me the honour of spending the rest of your life, with me?"

Feeling tears pooling in her eyes, she smiled. "Can there be any doubt?"

Sven took the tray away so he could hug her.

Breakfast suddenly forgotten in the excitement, the hug turned into them basking in their love for each other. He brushed her long hair off her face and gazed into her eyes. She loved him so. She brushed her lips against his and admitted, "This is the best day of my life, Sven."

"Mine too. I know my future will be brighter with you as my wife."

"What wonderful words for you to say."

"Each day I spend with you, I'm happy. Happier than I've ever been. When I'm not with you, I think of you all the time."

"Sven, remember when your cousin set us up?"

He loosened his embrace and stared into the depth of her soul. "How could I forget? When Anje called me, to announce that you'd meet me, I was so excited. I couldn't believe that an accomplished law student would agree to meet me."

"Why?"

"You're just so beautiful and elegant."

"Sven, you're making me blush."

"Now that we're engaged, our future together will be fantastic."

"You make me complete," she murmured.

They didn't see much of Montreal the rest of that weekend, other than going downstairs for an elegant dinner in the Opal's dining room. They vowed to each other to celebrate the day of their engagement in Montreal, in the same suite on the same date next year.

On the trip back to Newmarket, Sven drove while Kaitlyn kept stealing glances at her ring. Its design was compelling, yet simple. Sven had asured her that he'd chosen it himself. The ring was a bit too large, but she was bound and determined to wear it the whole way home, carefully keeping her finger crooked so it wouldn't slide off.

She was so happy, feeling strong and alive at that moment. Life simply could not get any better.

Sven dropped her off at her apartment. Following a rest, he carried on to Toronto. A hollow sadness overwhelmed her. The subject of cohabitation had not yet come up, and she didn't want to raise the issue prematurely. She was not opposed to the idea now that they were engaged, but she preferred that Sven broach the subject.

* * * *

Anje and her boyfriend, Mike, took Sven and her out to Scaramouche for a celebration of their engagement. It was a well-known restaurant that catered primarily to visiting celebrities. A lot of films were being produced in Toronto, and movie stars tended to gravitate to the restaurant that Anje had so carefully selected. She jokingly warned to keep a look out for a 'sighting', as if they were out bird-watching.

For that special occasion, Kaitlyn wore an amethyst-coloured sleeveless dress and coifed her jet-black hair in an elegant upswept. The only jewellery she wore was the diamond ring on her finger. Resized, it now fit perfectly. Anje even commented on the radiance about Kaitlyn and a genuine happiness that had not been evident during their time in law school.

Once seated, she gazed lovingly at her fiancé. She was so proud of Sven. He looked trim in his fitted suit, and the gold flecks in his tie brought on an intensity in his brilliant sapphire blue eyes. As if aware of her perusal, he gazed back at her as if he could devour her while he carried a gentle smile on his face. Throughout the entire meal, he was attentive to her every need.

Mike ordered a bottle of high-end champagne and, over oysters on the half-shell, they toasted the couple's engagement. An exquisite dinner of Cornish hen for Anje, Atlantic salmon in parchment with a lemon-dill sauce for Kaitlyn, pepper steak for Mike, and rack of lamb for Sven followed the appetizers. A decadent chocolate cake accompanied by strawberries and a rich vanilla sauce crowned the meal.

Sven took a bite of the cake. "Now this," he

smacked his lips, "is really good! I'm actually impressed."

"If you're impressed, then it must be way more than good." Kaitlyn reached and eagerly placed a sliver of the cake on her dessert plate.

After her last swallow of cake, Anje wiped her lips with her cloth napkin. "We have a surprise for you two."

"The dinner was enough of a treat, we don't need anything else," Sven protested weakly while glancing expectingly toward Kaitlyn.

"Anje figured we'd overeat," Mike cut in. "So we'd like to take you out to that nightclub, 'The Beat', in the entertainment district. Amongst their entertainment is a laser show. Occasionally, go-go dancers perform on pillars that go up and down."

Kaitlyn became a little concerned. "Aren't we over-dressed for this kind of place?"

Mike waved off her concern with a hand. "It's anything-goes. There'll be people dressed up, and then there will be hyper-skinny people dressed in the latest fashions. You may even see a few transvestites."

Sven turned to Kaitlyn with a what-do-you-think look. Kaitlyn shrugged, willing to try it out. Sven turned to Mike. "Sounds weird, but what the heck? Let's give it a whirl. It'll be an adventure."

The foursome soon found themselves standing outside the establishment in a line-up. They had waited roughly ten minutes when a limousine drove up.

Anje poked Kaitlyn in the ribs. "Look at the limo."

Kaitlyn turned to her friend and complied. They both craned their necks to watch a sleek and well-fed chauffeur open the rear passenger door.

"Do you think it's a Hollywood actor?" Kaitlyn asked, her attention glued to the open car door.

Anje gave her an anything-goes look. "Let's watch, discretely, so we don't look like dweebs."

A haughty-looking bald man exited the vehicle with a flourish. He looked around forty-ish and thoroughly bored, as if being dropped off by a limo was a daily occurrence in his life. Next, a waif-like, chestnut-haired woman emerged, wearing an outfit that looked like a creation by a leading designer. About ten pure silver bangles on her right arm chimed with her every move. She looked absolutely stunning, yet extremely young.

"Somebody is taking out their daughter." Anje giggled, giving Kaitlyn a little shove in the ribs.

"Yeah. Last year, he probably took her out to restaurants with a gym section so she could play with children her own age," Kaitlyn said in a low tone, laughing. She didn't want their boyfriends to overhear her nasty remark. But one glance at them confirmed the two men were talking guy stuff, and were totally engrossed in their conversation.

Kaitlyn shook her head. "I don't recognize these individuals."

"He's too ugly to be an actor," Anje snarled, obviously enjoying their nasty trend. "Maybe the girl is the famous party."

"She's pretty enough to be." Kaitlyn did admire her beauty.

The limousine couple walked past them, heading right up to the front of the line. Anje became flustered at their action while Kaitlyn tended an ear. The doorman didn't bat an eye and opened the door for them.

Kaitlyn turned to Anje. "Does Mr. Jordan ring a bell to you?"

"How'd you know his name?" Anje said, fuming.

Kaitlyn clucked her tongue. "The doorman said, 'Welcome, Mr. Jordan. Holly, good to see you again.'"

"They got right in." Anje bristled, not caring a hoot about their names. "Why are we wasting our time? We'll never get in at this rate."

"Let's give it another five minutes." Mike had picked up on Anje's rising temper. "If we're not inside by then, we'll go somewhere else." He patted Anje's arm lovingly, defusing her obvious resentment.

But then the line began to move along rather quickly and they got into the club. Inside, Mike escorted the group to an employee, tipped the man, and the foursome was admitted to the V.I.P. lounge, where they sipped on another round of champagne. Kaitlyn sighed with happiness. This was the good life.

The second level lounge overlooked the wide dance floor, over which multi-coloured laser beams made the dancers' movements look surreal. The black lighting had the dancers' teeth shine eerily as if lit from within.

Kaitlyn panned the room and caught sight of Emmy Award-winning actor Roy O'Leary, and his 'flavour of the month' girlfriend, sipping champagne at one of the tables. He kept admiring the back of his own hand while she gently gravitated back and forth in tune to the music. Searching for more celebrities, Kaitlyn's glance fell on the arrogant man from the limousine. Leaning against the bar, he poised a palm, and not delicately at that, on his girlfriend's neck, as if showing the world she was chattel.

A good tune came up, and Sven asked her to dance. They excused themselves and joined the throng of dancers. Mike and Anje remained behind, sipping their champagne.

At two in the morning, as if by mutual realization and acceptance, the foursome left the dance club by taxi and stayed in Mike's downtown condo. It concluded a memorable evening in celebration of their engagement.

Chapter Eight

Holly Nelson cowered in what her lover, Frank Jordan, called his panic place – a false space behind one wall of the bedroom of Frank's condo, approximately two feet deep.

"… check the place for his bitch … waste her too …" she heard through the plaster wall. Surrounded by countless kilos of marijuana, she clenched her teeth against a squeal that would surely give her away.

Two men, having hurdled the building's electronic entry code, busted in on Frank slumped into his recliner, listening to dance club music on his surround sound stereo.

Caught unaware, Frank had been unable to reach the panic place, but during the scuffle outside the bedroom, she'd dove for cover and secured the door from the inside. Now she was in darkness, straining to listen.

The stereo was abruptly turned up. She swallowed hard at the possible implication and her body stiffened. She dared not breathe.

Suddenly, two sharp thuds broke through the music.

Her body began to tremble. She looked down at her shaking hands and willed them to be still, but they wouldn't stop. Her body refused to obey her command.

Footsteps became clearer. The men had entered

the bedroom.

She recognized the sound of sliding doors. They were now rooting in the bedroom closet. The clink of clothes hangers and the rustle of clothing being chucked about confirmed her assumption.

Earlier, a business associate of Frank's, a man he addressed as Marty, had shown up unannounced for a none-too-friendly conversation about how Frank's life-style was drawing attention to 'the operation'.

She could tell that by Frank's humour turning sour, he'd been rattled by the drop. When Marty left, he ordered her to get ready. They would go out on the town.

She had been getting ready, and not happily at that, when the goons had entered the condo.

Frank had built the panic place himself and hid the entrance behind a pivoting chest of drawers. This chest of drawers was now a hair's breadth away from the men seeking her out.

A phone rang. Holly startled and slipped to the floor then gasped quietly. She froze. The phone in her bedroom rang again. A frightening pause followed. Holly had stopped breathing.

"You want me to pick that up, Wally? See if it's her?"

"Are you insane?"

Their silence seemed to last a lifetime. Had they spotted the panic room door? She went stiff as a board.

"Sorry, Wally, I wasn't thinking. She's not here, man."

Holly breathed a sigh of relief.

"Shit! Well, she'll turn up somewhere. And when she does …. Let's go."

Yes. Yes. Holly willed them out – out of the condo.

The sound of their footsteps waned, and a door shut, barely audible.

Just in case their leaving was a ruse to bring her out of her hiding place, she stayed put.

The glowing minute hand on her watch indicated that she'd remained trapped in her refuge for ten long minutes. What would she find when she came out,

Frank's lifeless body? She hoped they hadn't blown his brains out. What a mess that would be to clean up.

What was she thinking? She couldn't stay in the apartment with a dead man! She'd gather a spare change of clothes then never return to this dump.

What if they had someone watching the building entrance? She gave herself a mental shake. One thing she knew: she couldn't stay here.

She emerged from behind the fake dresser, crawling through the door into the bedroom. She rose, changed her mind about gathering a change of clothes, and crept silently into the living room, fully expecting a bullet in the head at any time. In the face of what confronted her, it might have been preferable. She'd never seen a dead body before, let alone that of a loved one.

She gave in to her horror and pain with great, strangled sobs.

Frank had toppled off the recliner, resting into a mess of skin, bone, and brain matter. One shot in the forehead and the other in his chest, near enough to the heart to have struck it, ensured that he wouldn't recover. Fragments of a bloody cushion with two-burn holes lay discarded nearby.

Panic struck her harder, deeper. She allowed herself one more thought for Frank, then returned to the panic room, grabbing the gym bag thrown near the chest of drawers.

Holly grabbed stacks and stacks of twenty-dollar bills from Frank's stash of untraceable cash he'd claimed, and stuffed the money in the bag. Feeling as if she might have enough, she reached and pulled on the only winter coat with a hood she owned, and went out the service entrance.

The winter wind sharpened her fuddled senses.

Frank's condo was a couple of blocks from Dufferin Street in Vaughan, a northerly suburb of Toronto. The nearest place for a fast getaway, she concluded, was the Yorkdale bus station. Holly flagged a taxi, a risky business on a wintry day, but a much quicker means of escape, less visible than public transit.

The taxi swerved to the curb. She got in, giving the driver her destination.

The driver was much too preoccupied with the nasty road conditions and his radio station's traffic updates to pay Holly much attention. She reached into her bag and pulled out two twenty-dollar bills in readiness to vacate the taxi. The drive seemed long, but then she wasn't thinking straight. She paid the fare and hurried inside the bus station.

Holly went straight for the departure board. The next outward bus was a local run to Sudbury, scheduled to leave in five minutes. *Great! That will do.*

Holly hurried to a ticket counter. She bought herself a ticket to Sudbury then sprinted to the bus platform, gym bag flailing against her thigh.

A few wet snowflakes fluttered from a pitiless black sky as the bus growled onto the northbound lane of Highway 400. It merged into a river flow of super rush-hour traffic. Less than an hour out of the most horrific situation of her life, she was surrounded by regulars with normal lives, commuting home to Aurora, Newmarket, and Barrie.

A terrible guilt enshrouded her. She had left Frank to rot in the apartment. She gulped on a sob. She couldn't have done more for Frank. Nothing at all, except to call 9-1-1. But then the police would have rushed in looking for a culprit. They would have eventually found the stash of drugs in the panic room. Where would she be then? In prison likely? No, she'd made the right decision by fleeing.

How could her life have gone so wrong, her life having begun so normally?

Born from loving parents in London, Ontario, Holly had enjoyed her first few years with her two sisters, Stephanie and Amber. She'd been cared for by her mom until Holly reached her tenth birthday.

Her father had died four years ealier from complications from cancer. Her mother had done a terrific job until one day, as she'd been driving home from her evening shift at the hospital. A drunk driver T'd the driver's side of her vehicle, killing her instantly. That night became a double tragedy.

The uncaring darkness, punctuated by the occasional light from a farm or country home, slid past, enveloped her in a feeling of twilit unreality. Irrational fears that the killers were already on her trail kept her awake.

Finally, the droning roar of the bus lulled her as she remembered the horrible day that changed her young life.

Their babysitter, Jasmine, had awakened her in the morning. Right off the bat, Holly knew something was wrong, very wrong, as Jasmine was always gone by morning. Then Jasmine had let in the church minister in and showed him to the front room. Once she and her sisters were huddled together, he delivered the awful news. He then explained with great care how she and her siblings would have to go into foster care because no family members were found to be living.

It had all been too much for one moment. Holly had never fully recovered. Holly and her sisters were to become Crown Wards.

After a hearing, Maxine Swayman, a lawyer, had told them that she would be advocating strenuously that they not be separated.

The Children's Aid Society worker, Violet Smythe, had gently guided Holly, Stephanie, and Amber into a courtroom within the old City Hall court system in Toronto while gingerly draping an arm over her twelve-year-old sister Amber's shoulder.

Holly was filled with dread. Violet had explained to them that they might be separated by the court system, and today's hearing would decide whether they would go to three foster homes or one.

Outside the courtroom, Maxine Swayman, their assigned lawyer, was waiting for them.

"Hi, Violet," the lawyer said, shaking Violet's hand. Then she lowered her gaze to her while Stephanie and Amber were taking in their surroundings. Ms. Swayman smiled at her. "I have good news. I have persuaded the judge to read an affidavit from a notable child psychologist Dr. Henry Yuri who states that it will be too difficult for the three of you to be separated. Hopefully, the judge will agree with the psychologist."

Overhearing, Amber turned and became excited. "So there may still be a chance, really? You're not just saying it to make us happy, are you?"

"No, Amber, there is a chance." Maxine smiled, but her smile waned quickly. "However, even if the judge agrees, Violet will have to find a foster home willing to take in three girls."

"If it comes to that, I will work tirelessly to keep these three together," Violet promised.

Maxine winked at the lot of them. "Well, hold tight until the case is heard."

Holly stared at Maxine's retreating back, a picture of elegance, with beautiful auburn hair and perfect clothes.

The case was called and the three of them, along with their social worker, were ushered into the courtroom. Holly noticed the neat rows of wooden benches and was affected by the serious mood of everyone present. She and her sisters were shown where to sit down. The case was read out, and Maxine Swayman stood to address the solemn-looking Judge.

"Your Honour, I represent the needs of the three minor children: Stephanie, Holly, and Amber Nelson. The girls came under the supervision of the Children's Aid Society when their mother, Tammy Nelson, died in a car accident, thus making them orphans.

"I strongly ask the court to ensure that the three minors stay together as they move from temporary foster care to become Crown Wards. The children have a strong bond, and it would be highly detrimental to their psychological health to be separated, given the recent trauma they have sustained."

The Judge nodded curtly. "I have read your brief, Ms. Swayman, and I believe in the legitimacy of your argument; however, it is an onerous task to expect the C.A.S. to find a family willing to foster three children all in one go." Holly grabbed Stephanie's hand in terror. The Judge continued. "I am prepared to rule on a six-month extension on the case in order for the C.A.S. to find a family willing to take in three girls. If the C.A.S. is unsuccessful at that point, then the children will have to be separated.

"Ms. Smythe, is your agency willing to work on such a placement?"

Violet Smythe stood up to answer the Judge. "I will personally do everything in my power to secure a permanent placement for these three minors."

"In that case, I will hear this case in six months."

"Thank you, Your Honour," Maxine replied.

The small family was escorted out of the courtroom as another family was ushered in.

In the hallway, the group stopped to talk.

"Girls, it's a half victory. If Violet can find a permanent placement, then you can stay together."

"We know, we heard," Amber said, eyes brimming with tears.

"I'll do my best," Violet assured them.

"I know you will," said Maxine and she concluded their brief meeting.

Holly watched her leave. The lawyer could walk with such a graceful manner.

As the bus rolled through the frosty night, Holly tried to remember meeting her foster parents for the first time. But all she could remember was that during the introductions, they were told that the Fransdons were a childless couple that had fostered many children over the years. The family set into a comfortable routine.

Through the years, Ed and Grace insisted that they had instantly fallen in love with the three girls, eventually adopting them.

Holly lived a safe existence; at least, until she became eighteen. Then, feeling the need for a change, for some adventure, she ran away to the city and couch-surfed with various friends.

Despite all the care the Fransdons had lavished on her, the feeling that she never really fit in lingered on.

She was an orphan. She carried such an ache in her heart for her real parents. This perpetual, corrosive emptiness within her remained through the years.

Soon after, she met Frank Jordan. This thirty-five-year-old petty criminal strutted with an allure of excitement that Holly quickly fell for. She wasn't attracted to Frank in a conventional way. His receding hairline and crooked teeth were hard to warm up to, but Frank wore expensive clothes and seemingly had an endless supply of money. He could easily provide for her.

Holly moved in with him when she had barely turned twenty-one.

As a gangster's girlfriend, she had to keep all of the knowledge about his businesses to herself. Time and habit dulled her morals and eventually she saw nothing wrong with her new lifestyle. Frank and she slept most of the day and partied most of the night. There were no boundaries. Holly never had to work, her biggest decisions becoming which clothes to buy.

Their condominium matched that of the square-footage of a normal three-bedroom house. Frank had paid for the services of an interior decorator to create a look of luxury. He drove a fancy car, a BMW, and when they went out to party, he always hired a limousine to drive them around.

Holly rearranged herself in her uncomfortable bus seat and reflected on how Frank had become more moody over the last month. He was always preoccupied with business, becoming almost unbearable to live with.

She never knew what would happen next. He was that unpredictable. Holly truly believed that Frank was nearing, or already suffering, a nervous breakdown. He screened all of his telephone calls, always took different routes when travelling, and increased the security to their condo.

His paranoia did him no good in the end; the two gangsters slipped into the apartment anyway and shot him like a dog. Luckily, Holly'd been looking for an outfit in the closet to wear to the party when the men broke in.

The bus took an exit ramp and turned onto a secondary road. A few kilometres down the road, it slowed to a stop, its air brake whistling, announcing its arrival at a small refuelling location called Waverley.

The village seemed to be little more than a post office, gas station, and a church. When the driver left the bus to go into the gas station to call on new passengers, Holly discreetly stepped off the bus and started walking down the nearest side road.

A fresh downfall of snow covered the ground. Holly trudged along the dirt road. Even in her depleted state, she could appreciate the beauty surrounding her.

The city with its dark memories was another life, another time.

Dollops of powdery snow hung delicately on the branches of evergreen trees. She allowed herself the luxury to laugh out loud. Her escape was wonderfully sophisticated in its simplicity. If Wally and the other hitman ever found out that she'd purchased a bus ticket to Sudbury, they would never think of searching a tiny village.

Luck was finally on her side.

The snow created an inviting canopy over the pine trees, and the full moon illuminated the roadway. But soon her toes ached from the cold. Her goal took shape. She had to find shelter to hide out from the elements.

Half an hour later, she spotted a shack not far from the road. She was out of options and nearly frozen. She left the road and investigated what was likely a hunting cabin.

On her approach, she noticed a generous pile of firewood in a lean-to right outside the door. That was a good sign. She peered through a side window, hoping .... She spied the wood stove. Holly renewed her search for a way in and found an unlocked window. She climbed in without any reservation. Finally, she would soon be warm, the first lap of her escape from the shooters complete.

Holly busied herself with building a fire, striking a match to old, dry newspaper. When a steady flame licked the kindling, she searched the rest of the homey cabin. Canned goods had been left behind forgotten. She didn't have a great variety, but she thanked the laziness of the person who left them behind. Holly found a can opener, ripped open a can of soup, and re-heated it on the wood stove.

She ate her soup with some over-the-hill crackers, pondering her current status as a fugitive. She was running from both gangsters and police.

She had no safety net.

Soon, a combination of sheer exhaustion and the need for mental respite sent Holly into the arms of Morpheus for the remainder of the night. She woke up late the next day. Nestled up in an old but serviceable sleeping bag; she emerged only to stoke the fire. God bless the folks who had left that woodpile!

In the early hours of her second night in the cabin, Holly formed the first clear concrete thought she'd had in months. If her parents had lived, they would be so disappointed by her lack of judgment and her general stupidity. Holly didn't want to dishonour their memory further, so she resolved to take action and come forward immediately. There was a terrible risk in her plan, but the time had come to do the right thing.

Chapter Nine

On the Monday following her engagement party, Kaitlyn returned to work. She concentrated on the cases under her care, yet she frequently found herself drifting off, daydreaming about Sven and their future together, until she met with Trevor Knight, another Assistant Crown Attorney.

Trevor had requested a meeting, claiming he needed her help, having four 'Driving Under the Influence' cases on his docket.

"Thanks for stopping by, Kaitlyn." He passed her a folder. "Here is the case file on an accused named Davis."

"What do you need me to do?"

"Would you review the case and get to know its details? I need you to ensure that all the reports are present in the file, and would you pass it on to Brenda Semple, the case administration officer?"

"Sure. I know Brenda well," she agreed, smiling. Kaitlyn liked Trevor, for his unbiased ways she had got to know from the dreadful episode at the pub.

"Brenda will then photocopy everything for Mr. Davis' defense lawyer." Trevor shook his head sadly. "You will get a lot of cases like this one, and this one is an especially good one for you to start with. Mr. Davis could lose his job and possibly everything he owns, if convicted. He would likely have to change careers, since the conviction stays on record for a minimum of five years. Only then could he apply for a pardon, but the pardon process can take another couple of years."

Kaitlyn nodded gravely. "I remember covering pardons at law school."

"Do remember that he chose to get behind the wheel and his decision is the reason we're here discussing his case."

"Good point. He should have taken a cab."

"Absolutely."

"If you have any questions, please come to me." Trevor chuckled as he rose and shook her hand. "Welcome to the zoo!"

The darkhaired, fair-skinned man of twenty-eight made Kaitlyn feel welcome with his kind smile and gentlemanly personality.

She returned to her workstation and worked on the file that she was assigned, with Brenda's cautionary message of keeping a balance at work well in her forethought. When lunch hour came, she sought the nearest park for a walk.

On this sunny spring the day was enhanced by the delicate, sprouting plants everywhere. Had the park been this beautiful last year? Kaitlyn had her doubts, but today she was happy to be alive and welcomed the challenges of her job. Even her salary was quite satisfying to her needs, which prompted a question on her present accommodations. Should she stay in her rental room, or get something more elaborate?

Kaitlyn glanced at the diamond solitaire on her left hand, like so many times before, and could not help smiling every time she laid eyes on it. She definitely was looking forward to a wonderful life with Sven, truly believing that she had met her true soul-mate.

After eating a sandwich and downing some mineral water, she returned to work and dove into her assignments.

A file clerk passed by her desk, wishing her a good evening. The intrusion startled her. Time certainly did funny things in this kind of work, like fly by. The rest of the week was, so to speak, a clone of that day; but daily, she still rose to the challenges that came at her without interruption or respite.

On Friday, she met with Marvin West, another

Assistant Crown. The brusque man wasted no time on pleasantries, assigning her some files and then dashing away.

West, she'd been told, had been at the Newmarket court for twelve years plus, and fully expected articling students to provide excellent work with little supervision. He despised sloppy work and held high expectations for anyone employed at the courthouse. He was by no means unpleasant, just abrupt.

Kaitlyn persevered, giving the senior lawyers what they needed when they needed it. Terry Ouellette assigned Donna McVeigh as her principal – a Crown to whom Kaitlyn could go to with any problems or for guidance. The assignment thrilled her. Donna, Ms. McVeigh, was an excellent prosecutor.

Although she didn't become overwhelmed, Kaitlyn spent the first three months in a whirlwind, struggling to please the Crown Attorneys while trying to balance her workload. She often returned from lunch to find new case files on her desk. It was a stern reminder that she must continue to manage her time effectively. None of the attorneys were difficult colleagues, though, and she learned something new from each one of them.

What most impressed Kaitlyn was the amount of time Crown Attorneys spent advocating in court. Donna McVeigh averaged thirty hours of court time every week in both the Ontario Court of Justice and the Superior Court of Ontario, while she balanced witness preparation meetings in a prominent murder case. Donna only had one jury trial scheduled in the near future, but she balanced over three hundred cases at different stages of development.

One afternoon, Kaitlyn sought Donna who confessed, "I really appreciate having a hard working articling lawyer like you in this courthouse."

"Oh … thanks," was all Kaitlyn could muster, so taken aback by the compliment.

"You're both efficient and astute enough to only bring the most compelling details or problems to me. Some lawyers take years to develop this skill. I'm really impressed that you already have a handle on this before you're even called to the bar."

Kaitlyn gave an appreciative smile. Working with Donna was such a joy. She hadn't wanted to interrupt her with unimportant details, forcing herself to quickly learn to think things out and 'prioritize' them before approaching her principal on case files.

Her chest filled with pride. It was paying off. Donna, a well-respected Crown Attorney, had taken notice of her effort.

Once she was well into the routine of her job, Kaitlyn concluded that there was no need to upgrade to a more luxurious place. The Marshalls, who owned the place, treated her like one of the family, occasionally inviting her for dinner. The children, Maggie and Matthew, were so busy in their activities outside the house that they rarely caused a commotion. Her rented room was almost quieter than living in an apartment building, plus she'd purchased a gym membership to a facility nearby and kept up with both her running and weight training.

Kaitlyn drove to Sven's place most weekends, spending what little time she could manage with him despite the fact that he worked almost every weekend. She enjoyed what time they had together. In addition to going out for dinner, they both enjoyed jazz and all its different permutations. They tried to go to a music venue every weekend to listen and relax. Anje and Mike sometimes came along as a double date.

Spending as much time as she did with Sven on her days off meant she didn't see her family as much, but the need to see them didn't wane. So in the fall, she rented a gorgeous suite, a short drive from her home, at the Markham Hotel, for Josh and her mom to stay in while they visited together.

Margaret hugged her really hard, saying she loved it. However, Kaitlyn noticed that its lavishness made Josh feel uncomfortable.

"Kiddo, all I needed was a bed and a bathroom," he said, shaking his head at what he referred to as a waste of money. But she insisted on treating. She noted then that he was trying real hard to make the most of it. The family checked out on the Sunday afternoon after a sumptuous brunch at the restaurant in the hotel. Josh confessed: "I could really get used to this."

"Can you boys put the luggage in the truck while Kaitlyn and I have a tea?" Margaret asked of the men.

"Sure, Margaret, we'll take our time," Sven assured her with a wink.

Once Josh and Sven left on the errand, her mom and she sought a table at the small café right next to the check-in counter. While waiting to be served, Margaret asked her, "Can you spare a weekend to come home and start planning the wedding?"

"Mom, we're going to get married only after I'm called to the bar, so there's no hurry."

Margaret patted Kaitlyn's hand. "My dear, we don't even know if you want to be married in Wanitou, or Harrisville, or Toronto. There's so much to do, especially if we need to book a hall."

"Mother, relax. There's no way I'd get married in Harrisville." She sighed. "I've always dreamt of being married with the rushing waters of Georgian Bay in the background, in a flowing dress surrounded by nature."

"Sounds lovely." Her mother smiled. "But what about Sven's family?"

The waitress approached their table, took their order, and left to get their tea. "Their interest lies in ensuring there is a lovely dinner following the service, but they're up for whatever we want."

"Even Wanitou?"

"Absolutely. I'll come home next month, and we can start planning. It will have to be in the autumn."

"Why?"

"I have fond memories of Georgian Bay in the fall with its vibrantly red and yellow-coloured maple leaves against the forest green of coniferous trees.

"Even as a little girl you loved the autumn." Her mom nodded. "I'll look into halls for the feast."

"Thanks, Mom."

"In the meantime, dear, you should think of a rain plan if it rains on your wedding day."

"Mom, you worry too much." The waitress set the two cups of tea on the table and quickly left to attend other customers. "We can always use the hall where the feast will be served, if it's that terrible; but trust me, the sun will shine, and the day will be heavenly."

Chapter Ten

The next morning, Holly was starved enough to leave the cabin in search of a more substantial meal. She walked back into Waverly, in search of any place that would offer food for sale. She spotted a local rundown motel that had a restaurant attached. Since the murder, she didn't think twice and finally devoured her first full meal, of four eggs over-easy, strips of bacon, whole wheat toasts while sipping three cups of coffee. After this extremely satisfying meal, she put in motion her plan and purchased a ticket on the next bus going south, to Toronto.

Holly arrived at the law office of Maxine Swayman and Associates without an appointment. Determined, she climbed the stairs to the second storey office and went straight to the receptionist's desk.

The moment the receptionist smiled at her, Holly inhaled a deep fortifying breath. "My name is Holly Nelson, and it's imperative that I see Maxine Swayman immediately."

The gate keeper of the inner sanctum checked her computer. She looked up at Holly. "You don't have an appointment, though."

Holly stared at the conservatively dressed receptionist. *She'll never understand how serious it is.* She forged ahead implying a connection. "When I was little, Ms. Swayman helped my family out in a child custody case. I know her. She'll help me."

"Ms. Swayman no longer practises family law," the receptionist stated.

"I know. She's a criminal lawyer, the best, and I need the best. It's an absolute emergency."

The receptionist assessed her. "You look cold, how do you take your coffee?"

Taken aback by the sudden reversal, Holly stared at the woman.

"Coffee. How do you take it?" The receptionist asked again to shake her out of her dumbfounded state.

"Black, two sugar, please."

"I'll get you a cup. Have a seat, Ms. Nelson."

She watched the receptionist disappear to get her coffee. Holly sought the most comfortable seat in the waiting room.

I hope she gets me Maxine. I don't want to talk to another lawyer, a stranger. She picked up a current copy of the Toronto Star and skimmed over its headlines.

"Ms. Nelson?"

Holly raised her glance.

"May I call you Holly?"

She shrugged. It didn't matter to her one way or another, providing she got to see Maxine.

"Here's your coffee." The woman smiled widely. She must have caught on her questioning expression because she added, "Relax, Ms. Nelson. Maxine will make time for you, today. It might take a few minutes for her to complete her present business."

An hour later, Holly was shown into Maxine's office. The lawyer prompted her to sit down. Holly was happy to hide the wringing of her hands.

Holly cleared her throat and began. "I don't know if you remember me, I am Holly Nelson and I'm in big trouble."

Maxine Swayman stared at Holly, seeking recognition. "Honestly, I don't remember. I've handled so many cases, I just can't remember them all."

"Over fifteen years ago, you helped my sisters and me."

"An adoption?"

"No. The courts wanted to make us Crown Wards, you argued the case to keep us together."

A look of recognition filled Maxine's face. "Right, right. Now I remember. Which of the three girls are you?

"The oldest."

Maxine nodded. "So, how can I help you today?"

Holly took a deep breath. "I am likely a suspect in a murder that occurred in Vaughan. I want legal counsel before I turn myself in."

"You must be terrified!"

Holly swallowed hard. "I am."

"All right then, do you want a coffee? You'd better tell me the whole story."

While sipping another cup of coffee, she related the events, and the lawyer furiously scribbled away.

Maxine raised a serious glance to Holly. "I'll set it up so we can meet with the police in Vaughan. I'll do all the talking, and you will only answer the questions posed to you. Do you understand?"

"Yes," choked out Holly.

* * * *

The meeting was set for five o'clock that day. The two women drove to the police station in ominous silence.

Maxine spared her a glance and inquired delicately, "If I can get you over this hurdle, have you considered where you can stay?"

Holly shrugged. "I figured that I would turn myself in and see what happens next. I'll probably be arrested."

"Since you fled the scene, you are likely right. I must be honest with you, it's not looking too good for you."

Holly stifled a sob. "I know." She stared out the passenger window, chewing on her lip.

Maxine spared her glances. She seemed to fish for words of encouragement but none did the trick. The remainder of the ride was ominously silent

* * * *

The interview at the police station started badly for Maxine's client. Constable Bryne, a crusty middle-aged officer with a slight Scottish accent, went at Holly as if interrogating a mass murderer. Dear Holly, following the instructions given, referred everything to her.

Maxine was anything but intimidated by the constable's tactics, having seen much worse. Nevertheless, Constable Bryne was going overboard under the circumstances. She stepped between the constable and her client. "My client has come in under her own volition. Do remember she is innocent until proven guilty."

"Okay, counsellor. I'll act civilized." He walked around her, and with a narrowed stare intent on still intimidating her client, he put his bulk in the nearest chair. "Very well, young lady, let's hear your side of the story."

As Holly explained the events, Constable Bryne at times stroked absently his jowls, but still listened intently, scratching notes in his weathered notepad. He would lay on impassive stares at Holly between his scribbling.

Her client finished relating the murder then sat stoically, not giving any extraneous details.

He slumped against the backrest of his chair, scratching at his beard shadow. "Why did you flee, then?"

Holly gave him an are-you-serious look. "I was scared out of my mind," she blurted with conviction, her fingers starting an involuntary flutter on the arms of her chair like laundry on a windy day.

"You say that, Ms. Nelson, but what makes you think that you could have protected yourself?" His voice and entire attitude somewhat mellowed out while he stared at her with what one might perceive as a hint of understanding in his eyes.

"Nothing." She shrugged.

"I find it highly suspicious that you aren't providing details of where you ran to or who you stayed with for the two days following the murder." Constable Bryne stared intently at Holly who now cowered.

"My client doesn't need to answer that." Maxine had foolishly misinterpreted understanding for conniving. She gave Holly a reassuring look.

"Well, Ms. Swayman, I do believe that your client panicked and ran away," he began with an unsettling certitude. "Once she realized that Frank was dead, she fled the scene to allow herself enough time ... to manufacture a story."

"My client has given her statement. Shouldn't you have your officers out looking for the real killers?"

"The real killer is in this room!" barked the Constable, leaping up from his chair. Then he abruptly left the room.

Holly slumped forward, burying her face in the crock of her arms and sobbed quietly. Maxine patted her back sympathetically. Being the cool lawyer, she remained poised and professional.

"Relax, Holly. He's playing a power and control game. The officer will return in a while."

Holly raised a tear-streaked face to her. "In a while?"

"He'll take his sweet time before he returns. It's a cop/lawyer strategy, which has nothing to do with you. Use this quiet time wisely. Put your head down and rest. Little does Bryne know that the rest will do you good."

"Sure." Holly nodded, smiling, seemingly reassured. She folded her arms and lowered her head once more, closing her eyelids. Maxine crossed her legs and leaned back, herself intent on catching a cat nap.

Constable Bryne took an entire forty-five minutes before returning to the interrogation room.

At the sound of the door opening and footsteps coming into the room, Holly and she straightened up.

The constable went directly to Holly and told her to stand. She obeyed with resolution. "Holly Nelson." At the pause, Maxine eyeballed her client, hoping she would hold up as Bryne said, "You have the right to remain silent ...."

Maxine gave her an encouraging nod and rose. "Holly, don't say another word to the police or to anyone, unless I am present, you hear?" Holly blinked her agreement. Maxine then turned to the Constable. "What is she being charged with, Constable Bryne?"

"First degree murder. Bail court will be tomorrow."

Chapter Eleven

On that very same evening, Anje called Kaitlyn, and once they exchanged the usual pleasantries, Anje got serious. "Kaitlyn, get yourself a copy of the Toronto Star, like, *tout de suite*."

"What's so special?"

"Remember that girl we were making fun of at the night club, the one shackled on the arm of the much older man?"

"The one that looked so young and pretty to be with such an ugly guy?"

"That's the one!" Anje sucked in a loud breath and went on, "She's on the front page, arrested for killing her boyfriend. There's a mug shot of him. It's him all right. He was the one with her at the nightclub."

A bout of the shivers shook Kaitlyn's body. "That's just so *creepy*."

"What's even creepier is that the murder happened in Vaughan. Isn't that in the jurisdiction of your court?" A silence followed, and Anje added in a wishful tone, "Maybe you'll be the one to prosecute her."

"Maybe I will, once I pass the bar," Kaitlyn said matter-of-factly. "Judging from how long the murder trials take to get through set-court dates, prelim trials, and pre-trial, I could be practicing for five years before this case gets to the court."

"It's still pretty interesting, no? Be even *more*

interesting if *you* got involved in it."

* * * *

The articling job terminated, and Kaitlyn returned to law school with its world of classes and examinations, of study and stress. Phase III of her law studies.

The examinations were tougher than ever before. Failure in an exam was followed by a second chance in that subject, but a subsequent failure resulted in repeating all of Phase III, bringing more cost in the equation and a delayed entry into the law profession.

Her study group re-formed again in a spirit of mutual support, unlike one cutthroat student who was found slicing pertinent pages out of a reference book in order to deny anyone else the information contained within. Kaitlyn studied all of the time, completely, at the expense of her social life but for the occasional evening with Sven.

Finally, the day arrived when the test results were posted on the bulletin board at the university. Kaitlyn walked to the immediate area of the board, stoically, feeling like someone on death row. However, before her was an enormous queue of students on the same mission.

What was on the wall determined the future of everyone, and it took a full ten minutes for her to reach the front. When under tension, Kaitlyn invariably had the urge to use the washroom, but there was no way she would leave the line, and so she held on, shifting from foot to foot, trying hard to ignore her throbbing bladder.

She came before 'The Wall' and scrolled down the student id number column in search of hers. She easily spotted her marks. Kaitlyn fought her wobbly legs and stifled an unexpected fit of weeping without success.

She'd made it!

Her outburst went beyond emotion. She would be called to the bar and would be a lawyer.

She was quickly elbowed out of the way and ended up at the periphery of the group near a bench. She slumped down, the commotion about her completely shut out. Finally, the assimilation was completed, and she gave a cheer under her breath, justly proud of her accomplishment.

Kaitlyn Wolfe was now a lawyer!

Chapter Twelve

Kaitlyn stood before her bed admiring the sapphire graduation dress that lay on the bedspread. She'd indulged five hundred dollars on the outfit. She still felt deserving of the expense for the most important day of her life to date. The ceremony of calling graduating law students to the bar would start in two hours' time. She turned to her full-length mirror and shed one tear as she remembered her dad's proud face.

The day John Lennon of The Beatles died from a gunshot wound on that fateful December 8, 1980, tainted the rest of her life.

She was running. Her Uncle Dwayne pulled up beside her and slowed his GMC truck to match her pace. "Hey. Do you need a ride?"

"No, thanks, Uncle Dwayne. I run every day for exercise and because I like the scenery."

"You're quite the runner. But you'd better get home." He gave her a cherished smile and he sped off.

Kaitlyn slowed her pace at the sight of an Ontario Provincial Police patrol car parked in front of her house. Normally, this wouldn't raise an alarm, but what puzzled her more was the second official-looking car. What was happening?

She rushed through the screen door and stopped dead. It took a moment for her eyes to adjust from the brightness outside to the dimness within. Detective

Sergeant Morton introduced himself to Kaitlyn from afar. The other detective remained nameless.

Both detectives stood before her mom who sat on the sofa with an ashen face and red puffy eyes. Aunt Jane was also present, keeping Nathan occupied while the adults talked.

Almost by instinct, Kaitlyn knew what had happened. All of her well-being feeling drained out of her body, to be replaced by a cold, empty numbness. She joined her mom on the sofa to hear what she knew was coming.

Detective Sergeant Morton looked directly at Kaitlyn, and began, "Your father, one of the finest officers I have ever known ..." Kaitlyn chest tightened. "... was fatally shot in the line of duty earlier today. We will have counsellors and social workers over this afternoon to help you, your brother, and your mom deal with this tragedy. Constable Wolfe was a brave man, and I am truly sorry for your loss."

She whimpered. She wanted to be brave for her mom, but needed her mother's strength at the same time. Such a complex feeling. Suddenly, on such a normal day, life could never be the same. Kaitlyn and her mom snuggled into each other wordlessly.

Once Kaitlyn's weeping eventually subsided to hiccups and a few involuntary shudders, she looked to Detective Sergeant Morton. "Did my dad suffer at all?"

"Your father received a fatal shot. He died immediately. Any pain would have lasted mere seconds," the quiet detective assured her with kind eyes.

"How did it happened?" whispered Kaitlyn fearfully to him.

The Detective Sergeant nodded to the other man. "Morton, please."

Morton straightened his shoulders and heaved a breath. "He stopped a vehicle for a minor traffic offense. Unbeknownst to him, the men in the car were armed robbers from Timmins. Your father came up to the driver's side, and the moment your dad asked for driver registration, the younger of the two men panicked and gunned him down."

"Did you catch the animals that killed my dad?" Kaitlyn demanded, her anger momentarily replacing her grief.

Morton shook his head. "They ditched the stolen car near Barrie. The men fled on foot. We have a national all-points-bulletin out for them, and hopefully, will have news of their whereabouts within hours. The fingerprints lifted from the car were quickly matched to known criminals. It should be just a matter of time. Our social worker and grief counsellor will be here any time now. She can help you much better than we can. We're just so sorry …."

"What does it matter?" Margaret wailed, coming out of her trance.

Jane approached Margaret. "It matters, it matters because you, Kaitlyn, and Nathan will need all of the support you can get right now for the next few months. The community will rally around you, as will the police. Everyone loved Clarence, Margaret, and everyone loves you and the children.

"You will not be alone. One of us will be with you, night and day, until you tell us you no longer need the support. We are your family and we love you. Everyone on Wanitou loves you. We will be there for you. We will be with you as much or as little as you want us to be, Margaret."

Aunt Jane leaned into Kaitlyn's mom, trying to comfort her, but her mom had returned to that trance-like state. She stared straight ahead and didn't move for the remainder of the day and night, dozing off on the sofa when her body claimed a rest.

* * * *

Over four hundred officers from the Ontario Provincial Police and the various Tribal Police Forces throughout Northern Ontario paraded at her father's funeral. It was a spectacular but moving affair, and the number of kind officers who took the time to speak to Kaitlyn and her mom overwhelmed her.

Her father had been a respected officer throughout Ontario, known not only to the O.P.P., but to members of the various regional and municipal forces as well. Even a couple of his police college classmates attended from the other end of the province.

After the funeral, the community put on a giant reception. It was a celebration of Clarence's life. First Nations drummers and dancers performed, and the police and the community were united in mutual respect for Clarence. In fact, unlikely as it may have seemed, the reception was the catalyst for many new friendships that day.

The older accomplice in her dad's murder was captured two weeks later, but he refused to turn in the younger man who had pulled the trigger, the real killer. The man, named James Booth, would ultimately receive a hefty sentence for both the armed robbery that immediately preceded the murder of a police officer. Somehow, though, it did not seem enough for Kaitlyn. She wanted a magic genie to turn back the wheels of time.

The endless stream of well-wishers and deliveries of homemade food began shortly after Jane's statement of support. Kaitlyn, Nathan, and her mom weren't alone for weeks, and the kind, gentle people of Wanitou supported Jane in her promise. The village became their extended family, and day-to-day tasks were handled in a compassionate and caring manner.

Jessica Grace, the grief counselor, became the foundation for spiritual healing, guiding her mom through the grieving process at her own pace. The First Nations community and the Elders used some of the traditional and spiritual ways to help with the grieving. Kaitlyn and her mom would have smudges and relaxed to the mellow smell of burning sweet grass.

Kaitlyn held her emotions in check almost too well when her mom slipped into her depression. She took on a mother's role; and although the community support was astonishing, she still had to assist her mom in her self care. Nathan bounced back exceptionally well, but still benefited from some special grief counseling for children.

Every evening, her heart ached for her dad. She could never forget the look on his face at the completion of her valedictorian address. It was the proudest moment she ever felt, and his tears of pride had only added to the pure joy of the moment. Clarence Wolfe had been a great father, and she would love him forever.

The combination of the therapy and the native rituals eventually broke her mom's despair. She woke up about four weeks after her husband's death, and, realizing that she had two vibrant living reminders of her husband, she hugged them both, claiming she was not going to let them down.

If dad were living today, he would be so proud of my accomplishment. I'm who I am because of my dad and those criminals who'd killed him. I'll be the best lawyer I can be and I'll have a strong conviction rate to honour my dad.

She tastefully applied her make-up and finished dressing, then put a final mist of hair spray on her coifed hair, professionally styled earlier that day. She was now ready for Sven's arrival to drive her to her graduation.

Miserably, Kaitlyn could only invite four people to the ceremony; a policy enforced by the university because of the sheer number of graduates. Kaitlyn chose Sven, her mom, her mom's partner Josh, and Nathan.

She arrived early and visited with her friends before the ceremony.

In a bout of exuberance, she hugged her best friend, shouting, "We made it, Anje, we'll officially be lawyers in a few minutes."

"It's been a hellova' journey and I'm glad we took it together," Anje said then smiled profusely.

"Yeah, me too," Kaitlyn admitted. "I wouldn't have made it without you."

Anje gave her the look. "Right." She shook her head in disagreement. "Kaitlyn, you're brilliant and it wouldn't have mattered who you went to school with, you'd have made it anyhow."

"I never would have met Sven without you."

"True."

"I think they're calling us to our seats." Kaitlyn took her friend's arm, and they filed in the hall.

When her name was called, Kaitlyn confidently crossed the stage of Convocation Hall to accept her certificate. A glance to her immediate smiling and clapping family told her that the moment was memorable in all of their lives. Sven, having borrowed a state-of-the-art camera, was snapping a close-up of her mom, hand to mouth and tears trickling down her cheeks.

Kaitlyn reached the dean of the law school. Her legs were wobbly, yet she held her shoulders back and smiled to the hundreds of people that filled the majestic hall, including her fiancé. Kaitlyn shook the official's hand and accepted her well-earned degree with pride bubbling out of her chest. Clutching her degree, she turned and smiled triumphantly at the crowd.

It's my moment.

Even the weather had co-operated.

Following the official ceremony, Sven ordered everyone to the gardens to strike a pose by the multicoloured flowers. The historical university buildings were the main setting, but in actuality, Sven said that he captured on film the heartfelt feeling of 'amour-propre'.

Time passed quickly, and soon everyone climbed into vehicles to reach Anje's house where a buffet awaited the graduation party and invited guests. It would crown the fabulous event.

Dr. Myers, the host, had connived with Sven to invite the study group, friends of Kaitlyn, and, of course, family members from their side. In total, sixty people came to feast on Sven's concoctions, a scrumptious buffet of both hot and cold items, champagne, beer and soft drinks, while all shared in Anje and Kaitlyn's graduation celebration until the late hours of the evening.

When complimented on his buffet, Sven would jokingly reply, "Lawyers gotta eat," which always brought on a round of applause. To Kaitlyn's assessing eye, Sven seemed uncomfortable at receiving compliments. Chefs worked 'behind the scenes' and accepting applause was an entirely new experience to him.

Josh Rice, Susan, Joe Charles, Buck, Leslie, Ida Waberay, and Nathan all attended, along with her mom. To everyone's vast amusement, Kaitlyn and Susan showed the crowd how they used to dance as teenagers in the eighties. Kaitlyn allowed herself two glasses of champagne, but the euphoria of being a *bona fide* lawyer had intoxicated her already.

She danced with passion, and being parched, Kaitlyn swept into the kitchen for some water. Josh, Anje, and many others from the study group had also pooled in the kitchen.

"It's the funniest thing I ever saw," Josh joined their conversation. "I was at the Wanitou Community Centre and two girls, oh about twelve or so, were bragging about you, Kaitlyn."

"Josh, don't keep me in suspense. What were they saying?"

"Well, the talkative one said that you were so smart that after ten years of university they were going to make you a judge right out of law school."

"Ha!" Anje interrupted, as if that could happen. She shook her head to clear the notion. "No free rides for you, Kaitlyn, even if you're smart."

Josh shrugged his shoulders. "There was no point in correcting them, Kaitlyn's a role model in Wanitou. I wanted them to admire her, even if they got the details a bit wrong."

Kaitlyn hugged Josh. "You're awesome."

* * * *

The following Wednesday morning, Kaitlyn received the break she needed to start practicing law.

"Kaitlyn? It's Terry Ouellette."

"Oh hi, Terry. Forgive me, I'm out of breath from a run."

"Good for you. Do you remember Joel Stevens?"

"Joel....he's one of your assistant crowns in Vaughan."

"That's why I'm calling. Joel has given his notice. He is going into private practice."

"You didn't expect this move?"

"I'd have to say so. Joel's explanation was that he's always wanted his own practice and feels that referencing his years as a crown will give him credibility."

Kaitlyn sighed. "And there's never a shortage of defendants," she provided, anticipating his next question.

"I automatically thought of you when the vacancy came up."

She wanted to dance around the room in triumph, but instead she used her well-honed calm voice. "Really?"

"Well, you did such a great job for us last summer that I hoped you would send us a resume." He paused. "You'll get the job, but we have to go through the formal process."

"The job posting will be available for any crown attorney in Ontario to read?"

"I'll be fighting to get you."

"Thank you, Terry."

"You are interested, aren't you?"

"Absolutely." Kaitlyn reigned in her enthusiasm, fearing she sounded like a schoolgirl.

"Send your resume directly to me and we'll give you a call."

She confirmed that she would, and Terry let her go, saying he had to get back to work.

She was granted an interview, and as she left the building, she felt confident that she'd done a great job. Despite her confidence, she worried ... about the competition, but surely her experience would catapult her to the top.

Three days after the interview, the phone rang. It was Terry.

"I'm calling personally to tell you that the job is

yours."

Kaitlyn's heart did a somersault. "When do you want me to start?"

"Yesterday." He went into a bout of laughter. "We'd like you to start Monday. Can you make it?"

"I'll be there."

Kaitlyn settled into her new role with zeal, carrying out her various assignments at a formidable pace. Not only had her year of articling prepared her for this role, she had nurtured strong alliances and connections in the courthouse. She was well-liked and respected.

The ink had barely dried on Kaitlyn's new business cards when Terry asked her to come to his office for a meeting. She sat down in the leather chair across from her supervisor.

"You take your coffee black, don't you?" he asked, and Kaitlyn nodded.

"Good." He extended a paper cup to her with a smile. "I picked one up for you on my way in."

"Thanks."

"You've acclimated yourself so well to this department that I'd like you to start handling cases on your own." He sipped at his coffee. "Your first case is an armed robbery with four defendants. The driver, a female, was allegedly one of the defendants' girlfriend."

"A real Bonnie and Clyde duo?"

Terry laughed at her analogy. "Well, he rolled over on her." He went into full-blown laughter at his unintentional double entendre. His fit of giggles finally subsided. "Clyde negotiated a deal and turned on his co-conspirators."

"No honour among thieves."

"Exactly. I'd like you to prosecute the driver, Bonnie. That is Becky Stone."

"Sure."

"She's managed to snag Maxine Swayman from Toronto."

It took all of Kaitlyn's strength not to react when Terry mentioned the Swayman name. "What's so unusual about hiring someone from Toronto? It happens all the time?"

"It's not the fact that she's from Toronto; it's the fact that she is a formidable opponent. I don't want to intimidate you, Kaitlyn, but in our circuit, she's referred to as 'The Barracuda'. Maxine Swayman is ruthless on cross examination, a fast talker but highly principled and intellectually brilliant."

Her excitement somewhat waned.

"Prepare yourself to battle against this woman and her associate, Taylor Robinson. A nice enough guy. We've been up against each other a couple of times. Taylor will likely do the bail hearing and the set-court date. He's one of those tree hugger naturalist types, but don't let his laid-back mannerisms lull you into thinking he's meek. He's a strong opponent. He'll handle all the early stuff, then Maxine Swayman will step in to handle the trial or the plea agreement, however it goes." Terry gave her an assessing stare. "Ready for this challenge?"

"Ready."

Her reply seemed to ease Terry's concern. "The case against Stone is clear cut. Harvey Smith, the boyfriend, had planned the armed robbery with two known felons, Fred Walker and Mike Sojourn. At his plea agreement, Smith disclosed that the hired driver, a previous cellmate, ended up in jail on the appointed day. So he needed a substitute, fast.

"Harvey went on to say Becky had berated him for hiring a loser for a driver so much that he became worn down by her nagging. He gave up and assigned her as the driver."

"A loose cannon?" Kaitlyn offered.

Terry went into a fit of laughter. Snickering, he added, "You have to hear this story; it's priceless. It turned out that Becky was a terrible driver. Four blocks from the crime scene, she ran a stop sign, instigating an incident with another vehicle. No impact resulted because the male driver from the other car was astute enough to slam on his brakes and stop a collision in time. However, Becky crashed the car into a mound of refuse sitting at the curb. The passenger of the other car, the wife, called in the emergency services on her cell phone, providing a partial plate number in the process. She related that the car scattered garbage over a wide area but fled nonetheless with refuse and re-cycling material still covering the hood and windshield of the car."

Kaitlyn was getting a visual of the entire scene and burst out laughing. "Go on."

Sharing a brief moment of laughter with Kaitlyn, Terry then sobered a tad. "The witness also claimed that Becky was laughing uproariously at the turn of events and didn't seem to know what to do. Then at the angry urging of the man next to her – that would be Smith – Becky drove away. These bright sparks then ditched the stinking car to steal another one.

"Harvey took the wheel this time, but the aging Monte Carlo kept sputtering and stalling as he attempted to drive away. Fred had hot-wired a lemon.

"The soot emerging from the car's exhaust and its beat-up appearance raised the suspicions of an officer from the York Regional Police who called in the plate.

"This is where the story gets even funnier. The license plate was registered to a Randy Masterson, a man with an outstanding bench warrant from another detachment. Although the bench warrant was for a minor violation, the officer was obligated to take Mr. Masterson in. The officer, William Humphries, called for back-up after having a bad feeling about the Masterson car, its driver and passengers. He followed the suspicious vehicle from a distance until the communications centre confirmed that another squad car was approaching their location from the other direction. Both police cars would intersect the suspicious car within the next block.

"They activated their lights to get the beat up car to pull over. But instead, the driver accelerated. The second police car boxed in the fleeing vehicle. The officers emerged from their cruisers and drew their weapons on the group. The four occupants of the car surrendered without any fuss.

"Constable Humphries received a commendation

for his role in the arrest and all four remained in custody awaiting trial. Harvey Smith squawked loudly on the co-accused at first opportunity, showing the man isn't honourable."

"I can just imagine the expressions on their faces when Humphries pulled them over. The lot must have been steaming," Kaitlyn commented.

"They didn't retaliate. I think the surrender was uneventful only because of the second police car at the scene." Terry let out a hopeless sigh. "Sadly, I think Becky Stone truly loves Smith; she sat in jail waiting for Harvey Smith to bail her out." He shook his head as if to clear his mind of the feelings he was harbouring. "She may be a victim of love, but she drove the get-away car, albeit only on its first leg. We need to hold her accountable. Here." He handed Kaitlyn the thick folder. "The rest is in the file."

"Thanks, Terry." Kaitlyn rose and picked up the folder. They ended their meeting, and she went back to her cubicle.

Once alone, Kaitlyn opened the file and read its contents, taking her own notes. Becky had a record for shoplifting and two B & Es (break-and-enters) from when she was nineteen. She had never served jail time for those crimes and had stayed out of trouble for seven years. She had survived mostly from a monthly welfare cheque, despite a valiant struggle to keep a job. She had worked at several donut shops on and off over the last seven years, but the notes in the file indicated that her lack of people skills was a constant impediment.

Becky could handle the baking aspect of the job with no difficulty, but whenever she was on cash or serving, she'd become flustered and made wrong change, slopped coffee, mixed up orders, and, society being as it is, irate customers would yell at her then she would quit. Not a helpful matter for an employment record as she would drift on to another dead-end job.

It was then that she met Harvey. The relationship developed with unusual speed and, in her desperation for security, Becky set up house with Harvey, after only one date.

Kaitlyn mentally agreed with Terry that it was a slam dunk to get a conviction. She prepared the disclosure for the Stone case, despite that it might be a couple of months before she actually met her opponent. She wondered how Ms. Swayman, dubbed 'The Barracuda', had aged since Stacey Cummings' case."

Swayman couldn't possibly be as tough as Terry made her out to be, could she?

Chapter Thirteen

Maxine arrived at the Newmarket courthouse early. The Crown Attorney, Kaitlyn Wolfe, was conducting the bail court that morning. Her research of Ms. Wolfe indicated she was a fair, thorough, and competent crown attorney despite her lack of seniority in the legal profession. She was not to be taken lightly. Maxine was not disposed to leave anything to chance.

She spied her adversary-to-be in the courthouse hallway. Ms. Wolfe was walking from the opposite direction, pushing a portable filing system with her cases for the day. Maxine recognized a self-assuredness in her bearing, like a ship under full sail. God, the woman was tall. She addressed her first, "You are presenting my client Holly Nelson's case in bail court today."

* * * *

Kaitlyn barely had time to register recognition and nod her head in acknowledgment before her opponent continued, "My client's name is Holly Nelson. Remember that name, she's not a killer. She's only still in jail because the detective-in-charge is too lazy or too incompetent to have found the real killers."

"Go on." Kaitlyn knew full well that Ms. Swayman would continue whether granted any time or not.

"Holly Nelson was hiding in a panic room of her

apartment when two assailants, possibly with connections to organized crime, came in and executed her boyfriend. She has relevant facts about the perps and needs to be listened to."

"Why did she flee the scene?"

"Survival." Maxine's tone of heavy patience that one would use with a dull child irritated Kaitlyn. "She heard one gunman tell the other that she would be snuffed out next."

"Really!"

"You should hold her as a material witness and not a defendant," Maxine added.

"Aren't we getting ahead of ourselves here?" Kaitlyn took strong exception to the Swayman woman's lecturing tone. "You should ...." She narrowed her gaze at the woman, showing her disapproval. "What is her safety plan if released?"

"We were approaching the issue when Constable Bryne arrested her."

"She's safer in jail if there are possible connections to organized crime."

Ms. Swayman shook her head, adding, "I don't think so. We don't really know who we are dealing with here just yet, plus organized crime has tentacles in the jail system as well.

"I will consider your words once I have a senior homicide detective talk to your client and report to me." Kaitlyn confirmed her decision with a curt nod. "I'll seek out having her held at the bail hearing and, instead of her being transported to Metro West for processing; I'll have her returned to the holding cell pending a meeting with one of them."

"Okay by me. When can we meet after you get your report?"

"I'll try for later today. In my office?" At Ms. Swayman's nod, Kaitlyn instructed, "Second floor."

"Thank you," Ms. Swayman said and both lawyers parted in their own way.

Maxine Swayman .... 'The barracuda' was the very same lawyer who had gotten Stacey Cummings a sweetheart deal when her nemesis had nearly killed her with a spiked drink. This case would have personal overtones, and Kaitlyn resolved to give Ms. Swayman a ride she would never forget.

* * * *

Maxine was unable to talk to her client before the bail court. The would-be killer was led into the courtroom with four other defendants. They were quickly settled in an enclosure of Plexiglas. How pale and worried Holly looked. Maxine tried to catch Holly's attention, but all her client could do was stare blankly at the floor, a figure of utter dejection and hopelessness.

After court was officially opened for the day, Ms. Wolfe rose and called out Holly's full name. Holly rose as per the bailiff's instructions. As her lawyer, Maxine also stood up.

The Crown, Ms. Wolfe, then addressed the judge. "Ms. Nelson is charged with murder. Her whereabouts during the two days after the death of her common-law husband are unaccounted for. I would like her remanded without a chance at bail."

As defence attorney, Maxine then had a chance to refute. "Your Honour, I represent Ms. Nelson. My name is Swayman, spelled S-W-A-Y-M-A-N, first initial M.

"Ms. Nelson doesn't have a police record. She had the misfortune of having been in the apartment when her life-partner was executed by two men. She came forward of her own free will and presented a statement to the police. Ms. Nelson is not a flight risk. She's unemployed, without ties to any other community and has no financial resources."

The Judge turned to Holly and gave her an appraising stare. "Ms. Nelson is remanded to custody until the sixteenth of next month. Bail is set at $50,000."

"My client doesn't have the financial resources to meet that obligation," Maxine interceded.

"Sorry, Ms. Swayman, but that amount is firm." The Judge put the case folder aside and raised his glance to the court services officer. "Next case."

Ms. Wolfe cut in. "Your Honour, one amendment please?"

"Yes?"

"Could Ms. Nelson be held at the Vaughan police station until the first court date, instead of the regular jail?"

"On what grounds?"

"Holly Nelson has informed her lawyer that she overhead the alleged murderers swearing to kill her. I seek an opportunity to meet with Ms. Nelson to personally determine if she is a victim or a defendant. Your Honour, she will be much safer at the police station until a meeting can take place."

"I will give you some leeway on this one. Amendment is granted. Next time, present all details before the defense presents. Understood?"

Chapter Fourteen

Over a week after Holly Nelson's bail hearing, a slight, blond haired woman de-trained at the institutional green-tiled Toronto Wellesley subway station. She panned around, searching for the exit sign.

Becky Stone rode the escalator up to the street level.

The woman with iridescent, watery eyes and enlarged inky pupils found her bearings and walked as far as Gloucester Street. The street went only one way – to the east – so she quickly figured out how to find her destination. Another five minutes of brisk walk lead her to the building with the sought-after brass plate on the door: Maxine Swayman and Associates.

Becky Stone negotiated the stairs to the lawyer's suite of offices and opened the reception door into a sitting area that mirrored one of *The Young and the Restless* or another such show. Needing to relax after her long walk from the subway station, she hoped the lady lawyer would be late.

She approached the receptionist. "I'm Becky, here to see Ms. Swayman," she said avoiding eye contact.

"Ms. Stone, yes, I have your appointment. I am Lillian, Ms. Swayman's office manager. She will be with you in just a few minutes. In the meantime, would you care for a coffee?"

"Oh, please, yes. A double, double."

Becky sank into a leather sofa, surreptitiously massaging the soft and wonderful fabric. The piece of furniture must have cost hundreds of dollars. She settled into a daydream about owning similarly gorgeous things and nodded off while her coffee grew cold. She was startled ten minutes later by the receptionist calling her name. "Ms. Stone? Follow me, please."

Lillian ushered her into an office, which had more rows of books covering the walls than anything that she could remember from the library at her high school. As the lawyer introduced herself, Becky was stunned at her attractiveness. She was small-boned like herself, with red hair that looked regularly styled by a hairdresser. Lawyers had to make a pretty penny.

"Did you have a hard time finding the place?" the lawyer asked her.

"Oh, yeah. Once I reached the street, I was lost." Becky struggled against her slight lisp. "There are tons of cars drivin' by around here and the hot dog vendor was yelling to people to buy his stuff, and the people rushed by didn't ssseem friendly at all. It was all so scary."

"But you managed to find my office building."

"I concentrated then I remembered the words of my sssocial worker, 'Walk to Yong Street, turn right, and walk some more.' "

They exchanged pleasantries, after which Maxine Swayman became all business.

"Please tell me about the events which led up to the crime."

"Harv cut down on his drinkin' which made him miserable. He called it his ultimit chance. He made planss every day, and if I got in hiss way or made noise cleanin' when he schemed, he would beat me."

"What do you mean by that? In what manner would he beat you?"

"Cuff me around the back of the head, which he ssaid wouldn't matter on account of me being a retard and all." Becky sniffed, averting eye contact. "He'd hit me where nobody at work would see the marks. He was real tense for the weeks before the robbery and I did a lot of things wrong by Harv."

"Like?"

"Well, like after working hard baking donuts all day, I'd sometimes get lazy making his meal." She shrugged. "My job to make the meals. Make 'em right. Once, I burned hiss hamburger on account of my soap opera and he decked me. I deserved it, too."

Oh, oh, thought Maxine, Stockholm syndrome or.... Poor soul actually thought she deserved such treatment. Sighing, Maxine put the thought aside; that was another matter altogether. The woman had such a distracting speech impediment that she had a hard time following the conversation. Maxine gave herself a mental shake. Time to focus.

"Let's move along to the planning of the robbery."

"Yeah, yeah. Harv knew these three guys from doin' time in Milton. Freddie, Mike, and Rodent. Rodent was his street name on accoun' of him looking like a rat. Never really knew hiss real name." She shook her head in confirmation. "Never did. Rodent was suppos' to drive that day, but he didn' show up. Harvey found out that Rodent was in the tank then smacked me for Rodent gettin' all wasted up and getting thrown in the drunk tank on accoun' of it bein' ultimit chance day and all.

"Anyway, I had to be the get-away driver just like on the TV. Never did see a lady get-away driver on my soaps. Do you watch the soaps? I know all about them, ya know."

"Let's stick to the story," Maxine said kindly. She had neither time nor inclination for the soaps.

"Oh, yeah, yeah. Anyway, Freddie, Mike, and Harv went into the bank and they were back in minutes. They hooted and hollered and Harv ordered, 'Drive.' Well, I drove but I gotted all confused. The doctors say I have a learnin' disability, but Harv just says it's cause I'm retarded. Anyways, I didn' see the stop sign until it was too late. Harv yelled, 'You stupid bitch.' I tried to avoid hittin' some fancy pants' car." She sighed deeply. "I messed up like always and hit 'em. Stinking garbage everywhere!" Becky swung her arms out, indicating a huge mess. "I started to laugh on account it was a funny sssight. Harv then pointed to a car; a Monte Cristo, no a Monte Carlo or somethin' that rhymed with that. He told me to drive to it. Harvey drove, and then ten minutes later, the cops cornered us and we all got arrested'.

"That'd be the whole story. Except they put me in jail and I didn' get to see no TV for two days! One of them free lawyers that the court gives ya, think he was called a duty council lawyer, done the bail hearing and they let me go home, 'cept I don' have a home no more. Harv had somebody change the locks so I could't get in. I went to a homeless shelter. They got me to see you." Becky choked up. "I hear from friends that Harv's out and he got himself a new woman."

"Did you have anything to do with planning the robbery?" Maxine prodded.

"No, ma'am."

"How did you end up being the getaway driver?"

"I was at the donut shop and Harv comes in and tells me I'm sick and I got to leave, so I told my boss and Harv dragged me out."

At Becky's silence, Maxine prodded more. "Did you get angry at Harvey because the robbery might not happen?"

Becky shrugged nonchalantly. "No, I didn' care."

"You were the driver of the get-away car."

"Harv told me I had to be the driver! I telled him that I don't have no license."

"Okay, so why did you drive?"

"Lady, you don' refuse Harv nothin'. If you ever back-talk to him, you get a whupping. Also, him and the others had guns and I wasn' saying no to any of them, you understand?"

Maxine nodded in understanding. "Okay, let's have a look at your previous convictions. You have two break-and-enter convictions and one shoplifting."

"Well, another man-friend of mine, he made me do a few 'B & Es' for hiss kicks. He said it'd get him all hot to see me wearing all black like a character from the TV and breakin' into people's places. I loved him, so I did what I was told. Afterwards we'd drink wine and smoke and laugh at the ugly houses we broke into."

"And the shoplifting?"

"I was broke and I wanted something pretty! So I put a scarf under my jacket and I walked to the door. Darn thing had itself one of those security tags on it, so I beeped when leaving the store and got arrested."

"Your file says that you had seven years where you weren't in any trouble with the law."

"Yeah, my man dumped me and no one wanted me on account of me being sstupid until Harvey came along. He's the best man I ever had, ya know."

"Becky, he's trying to say that you forced him to do the crime by nagging him."

Maxine's client dismissed the notion with a wave of her hand. "He don't mean that. He's just mad cause I screwed up by wrecking the first sstolen car. Just you see, he'll come back to me cause he loves me. You'll see. The new chick won' last long with Harv."

"We can explain to the judge the circumstances. I've read the Crown Screening Form. Becky, they want you in jail for five years for your part in the robbery." At Becky's alarmed look, she added, "But I feel we can fight it."

"Good 'cause I'll be too old to make babies after five years and no man will want me then, ever."

Maxine sighed at the desperation of the woman. "Did you speak to the police or anyone in jail?"

"I know from my man-friends not to talk to the cops, so I didn't. In jail, I was so scared, I didn't even talk to other girls, not at all."

"That's very good, Becky. Your first appearance date is in four weeks. Listen to me." Becky focused on her. "You will plead not guilty, and I'll work on your defense."

"Thanks, lady."

"Are you working with the social workers to find a place to stay?"

"Yeah, but I don' make good money making them

donuts, I only make minimum wage, so it's not easy, but I'm trying. The rents in Toronto are too much for me." Becky shook her head miserably. "The social workers had me apply for disability on account of that learning disability, and on account of me getting fired so much cause I don' always remember things right, not at all." She shook her head to confirm her words.

"If you move out of the shelter, let Lillian know." Maxine gave Becky a business card. Becky nodded and confirmed that she would do as told.

"When I leave your office, do I go right or left to get to the Wellesley Station?"

Maxine stared at Becky, "Left to Yonge Street. Once on Yonge, you'll see the station at Wellesley Street."

"It's that green station, right?"

Chapter Fifteen

Kaitlyn's eyes blurred as she read and re-read the case file on Harvey Smith, Becky's estranged lover. She had the case file on Becky Stone open as well.

Harvey had retained his lawyer the day he was arrested and negotiated quickly with him. He renounced any major role in the crime, claiming that Becky, Maxine Swayman's client, master-minded the entire operation, an assertion his lawyer took to the Crown Attorney's Office. Records showed that Becky stayed quiet throughout her two days in jail. The duty council lawyer's scribbles indicated that he had serious doubts that Becky really understood the legal system from his talks with her.

Becky had been released on bail with some fairly stiff conditions, including weekly probation meetings, not leaving town without notifying the court, and she could not change her address. Once she was homeless, Harvey's lawyer tried to make her look like an irresponsible transient who could not even keep a fixed address.

The other two robbers, Mike Sojourn and Fred Walker, were looking at lengthy sentences for armed robbery and were equally anxious to have their lawyers plead down the case.

Mike Sojourn had spent most of his adult life in and out of jail, and didn't seem too worried about the idea of going back in. He retained the same criminal lawyer who had represented him for all of his previous crimes.

Kaitlyn came to a copy of a police report attached that confirmed someone had sought out Rodent, and beat him up for messing up the get-away plan. The report also mentioned Mike hadn't sought out Becky, his explanation being he'd never beat a woman, that he had been taught that much from his mother.

What disturbed Katilyn was the report also claimed that Mike had ranted that he wanted to beat Harvey but didn't because he knew how connected Harvey was, which supported Ms. Swayman's words.

Having been present at his bail hearing and that of Fred Walker, Kaitlyn had witnessed plenty. Mr. Sojourn's lawyer seemed perturbed that he had to go north of Toronto for a case. She overheard Mike wanting to plead guilty as soon as he could and expected his lawyer to work out a good plea bargain for him. That way, he'd be out of the joint by the time his grandson was three so he could then start the little guy on playing ball. If it weren't for his grandson, due to be born soon, he just wouldn't care and would warm a cell for as long as he had to.

On the other hand, Fred Walker, twenty-six, had only one other conviction, a break and enter in a Toronto home. His greatest vice was greed. He willingly participated in the robbery because he admitted he wanted the cash to pay down his gambling debts. Fred seemingly had delusions that he would beat the conviction in spite of what his lawyer had told him. Reality and Fred Walker were distant fourth cousins, destined never to meet.

Hearing footsteps, Kaitlyn raised her glance to see the night security guard walk by her desk on his round. It was after midnight. She stood up and stretched, took a walk up and down the corridor, then after downing another stale coffee, she resumed her reading.

The case history went on to show that Harvey Smith had returned to his apartment with Mary-Jo, his new girlfriend, and awaited his sentencing. He had to report to his probation officer for a sentencing report; but otherwise, he just stewed in the apartment and had Mary-Jo cook all his meals. He claimed that Mary-Jo held no real loyalty toward him and knew he would be going away for at least four years because of his stupid ex-girlfriend. He admitted that she needed the free room and board and that he used her for sex. In his mind, it was a balanced relationship, as neither of them had any expectations for the future.

* * * *

Taylor Robinson, an associate lawyer in Maxine's firm, sat across from her for a meeting in the conference room on a dreary Monday morning. Two mugs of coffee steamed as they went over some of the pending cases.

"What about the Becky Stone case?" Taylor asked Maxine.

"I'll get you to do the first appearance on it. It'll be held at the Newmarket courthouse on the twentieth of this month," Maxine said. "She is charged with both conspiracy to commit armed robbery and armed robbery."

"Dear God," Taylor said, his eyes widening. "She doesn't do things by halves, does she?"

"She sure doesn't. Poor soul is certainly not the sharpest knife in the drawer. You really need all your marbles to follow her in a conversation."

"Terrific." Out of frustration,Taylor slumped against the back of his chair.

"She wants to plead not guilty. This will buy me time to work on a defense."

"What are the specifics of the case?"

"Becky is a woman with a severe learning disability who was bullied into being the get-away driver in an armed robbery orchestrated by her abusive partner, a real charmer named Harvey Smith. His lawyer got to the assistant crown first and he plead down to the use of a firearm in the commission of an offence.

"Harvey claims Becky was the ring-leader and once you meet her you will see just how preposterous that idea is."

"Because of her—"

"She could not form the intent to plan the crime. She has difficulty maintaining a menial job at a doughnut shop. Her social worker even corroborated as to just how difficult it was for Becky to find us by subway."

"Poor thing."

Maxine nodded. "According to the records, when she stays away from abusive men, she manages well. Becky has such low self-esteem that she is a magnet for the most disreputable men. She once had a partner who made her dress up like a television character, and they committed break and enters together."

"Dear God." Taylor shook his head at the extent that men would go with Becky. "Does she have *anyone* on her side?"

"Not as far as I can tell just yet. She is currently living in a homeless shelter. One of the workers there is trying to help her with managing her finances and finding her a home. We didn't talk about family. I don't believe she has any family supports."

"Dear God," muttered Taylor again.

"Rarely do I feel sad for a person, but in her case, I really do. She really has had a hard life."

Taylor pulled out another dossier from his briefcase and opened it on the desk. "The newspapers are really eating up *this* case."

Maxine caught sight of the newspaper clipping with a prominent picture. "The Jordan murder with this very young and very pretty defendant." Of course, it was Holly Nelson. Maxine gave him a teasing smile.

Taylor crossed his arms. "She's beautiful and not the air-headed party girl that the newspapers are making her out to be."

"I agree. It's a weird case. She is a strong witness, and I'm sure that the prosecution doesn't have a clue."

Maxine filled Taylor in on the specifics of the case and instructed him to conduct an investigation on Holly's background to ensure she wasn't profiting financially from Frank Jordan's death. The two lawyers went over six more case files, and then Taylor retired to his office to get on with the day's work.

Chapter Sixteen

The first appearance date for Becky came up four weeks later, for which Taylor took the forty-five minute drive from his downtown apartment to Newmarket.

Taylor arranged with the shelter's manager to meet Becky Stone at the court. A worker from a community outreach program would attend all of the court proceedings with Becky in order to provide emotional support and help further explain the events as they unfolded.

Of Newmarket, he had an almost identical impression as Maxine's. The interesting community fostered a balance of affluent homes, subdivisions of newly built single-family homes, and a full array of amenities. These types of areas were where normal people sought to reside – the kinds of people who spend their free time helping the kids with sports or in going to the library.

Taylor had real admiration for community-involved people and had no use at all for those who were blind to the sufferings and shortcomings of the world. He spent his own free time trying to make systemic change through a non-militant poverty coalition, arduous but rewarding work. The more you put into life, reflected Taylor, the more you got out of it, and it was from a particular compassion for those such as Becky that Taylor looked especially forward to this case.

He entered the courthouse and the activity inside was at the usual frenetic pace of any other courthouse. Taylor located the courtroom for the correct Ontario Court of Justice where the proceedings were scheduled to occur. In front of it, a large waiting room held a crowd of over sixty people sitting or standing. Any more and the officers of the court would have insisted that others wait outside the courthouse.

Taylor quickly spotted two women, a petite, washed-out blond with blotchy skin and a kind-hearted looking woman. He suspected they were his quarry. He approached the one he suspected was the defendant. "Would you be Becky Stone?"

"Yup."

"Hi, I'm Taylor Robinson." He reached out and shook her hand. "I'll be representing you today." He then turned to the other woman. "And you are?"

"I'm Lauren McRay, Becky's outreach worker." She gave him a wide smile. "I recognized you from the University Avenue courthouse."

Taylor returned the smile. "It's my second home."

The two laughed, but the humour seemed to be lost on poor, confused Becky. Taylor waved them out into the hallway to talk, and in the discussion, he ensured that Becky understood what would transpire that day. He secretly sighed in relief; Becky seemed to grasp his explainations. With Lauren present, the proceedings would be easier on Becky.

"Do you think Harv will be here?" Becky's whiny but wistful tone tore at his heart.

He shook his head. "My notes indicate that he has already been found guilty and is awaiting sentencing. Didn't Maxine explain that to you?"

"I guess. I didn' get it then. I didn' get it at all, not at all."

Taylor asked Becky to quietly point out the other co-accused. Fred was nowhere in sight. Taylor surmised that he may have pleaded guilty.

The court proceedings began promptly at ten that morning. The court clerk called Becky's name after only nine other cases, the last being of Mike Sojourn's. His lawyer had acquired a remand of the case for forty days. Taylor requested the same for his case since they were related and thus increasing the likelihood of success. For an explanation, he apprised the Judge that they were just retained and needed more time to build a defence.

While Taylor awaited the Judge's decision, an unusually tall and efficient-looking assistant crown attorney working on the case snagged his attention. He'd been cautioned of her; she was known to work her way through the files efficiently, approaching each one as if there were no others.

The Judge remanded his case until the same date as that of Mr. Sojourn's. After court, Taylor guided Becky and Lauren in the hallway. He then explained to Becky in simple terms what the future held. "Basically, Becky, you will have to come back to court for the Judge to set a date for trial."

Lauren asked, "Can I attend in order to support Becky?"

"I would really appreciate if you could," Taylor replied, and Lauren confirmed that she would through a genuine smile. Meanwhile, Becky stared down the corridor, likely expecting or hoping to see Harvey.

Lauren caught Becky's arm. "You'll have to come back to court. Do you understand this?"

Becky whipped around to Lauren. "What?"

Taylor explained once more. "The Judge has given us time to build a case for you, but you'll have to come back to court with Lauren to set a date for trial." Frustrated by her absentmindedness, he asked, "Do you understand?"

"Yup. Me and Lauren come back and my name gets called up. I come to the front, and he sets a date for my trial. Will Harv be there?"

Lauren sighed, obviously loosing her own patience. "Becky, this case is about you. Remember, your lawyer said Harvey has already pled guilty."

"Oh yeah, yeah. I forget. Will you drive me here, Lauren?"

"Of course."

"Thanks. I could never figure out the buses in Vaughan from the homeless shelter. It would be too much for me."

"Ladies, bring a book, bring a snack, and prepare to be here for the full day. Occasionally, the crown will let defendants represented by council go first, but there are no guarantees."

"I'll make sure Becky is here."

"Thanks," Taylor said and he departed.

* * * *

Taylor had an all-news radio station blaring on his drive back to the Toronto office. The lead story was about a paramedic who, having just finished his midnight shift, was sleeping in his suburban Markham townhouse. A strange noise in the man's living room woke him up. The man got concerned as the noises went on and groggily grabbed an alarm clock, the closest weapon to his bed. He had then crept downstairs.

An intruder had broken into his home. The off-duty paramedic confronted the un-armed robber, striking the would-be robber with his only weapon – the alarm clock. He then called the police and held the intruder until police arrived. The thief refused to divulge his name and did not carry any identification on him.

Taylor went into a fit of laughter. The only reason the radio station was running the story was due to the battery-operated alarm clock, which came on to the station reporting the news when the homeowner clouted the robber. The news reporter closed up his report by saying that after running the thief's prints, the perpetrator turned out to be twenty-six-year-old Fred Walker from Toronto.

Hearing the name set off his hilarious laughter. A Fred Walker was a co-accused in Becky Stone's case; could it be the same individual?

Chapter Seventeen

After completing court at 8:00 in the evening, Kaitlyn was totally drained of energy. First appearance dates could be such a zoo. Hearing from over one hundred defendants in one sitting was daunting.

An Assistant Crown Attorney within their office approached her at her cubicle, introduced himself, and inquired about her day.

"Hi, Trevor." She gave him a brief smile and went on, "I had a twenty-two-year-old kid on my docket today. He came to court in a leather jacket with clothes that looked slept in. I've seen him three times already for various charges."

Trevor had a deep belly laugh at her expense. "You'll see some of the accused multiple times for multiple charges. That's why a good sense of humour is a must in our profession."

"I have a good sense of humour, but I can't see how a twenty-two-year-old can be that messed up."

Trevor sobered and shrugged. "It happens all the time." He paused then asked, "Did you have a defendant named Walker today?"

"Yes, but he no-showed."

"He had a reasonable excuse." At her dubious look Trevor gave her a deadpan look.

"Yeah, right."

"Walker was busy breaking into a Markam home.

The owner caught him red-handed and hurled a radio at him. Only after running his prints did the authorities identify him as Fred James Walker."

"You're messing with me!"

"I'm dead serious. It's all over the news. I checked it out. I happened to see your docket this morning because of some confusion between our cases and I glanced at that name. I wouldn't have remembered it, except I have an uncle named Fred Walker from Calgary."

Kaitlyn gave him a curt nod, letting him know that she appreciated knowing of a detail that could affect her case. They stood in silence for a brief moment then she had an idea. "Have you ever heard of a defence attorney named Maxine Swayman?" She wanted to know all she could of the tactics Ms. Swayman was likely to use against her.

"No, should I have?"

"Not really. One of her clients is in my courtroom. I've been told that she is extremely tough to deal with."

"Where does she practice?"

"Downtown Toronto."

At this detail, Trevor lightened up. "I've got a buddy at the University Avenue courthouse, I'll ask him about her. You have nothing to be intimidated about, though. You're sharp and tenacious."

"Thanks for your vote of confidence, Trevor." He gave a two-finger salute and walked away. "See you tomorrow," Kaitlyn called to his retreating back.

After entering final notes on the brief she'd been reading, Kaitlyn drove home. She listened, first hand, to the odd story about Fred Walker. At her apartment she gulped a microwave fettuccini dinner and propped herself up in front of the television until the late news came on. The clock-radio story made the news once more.

The phone rang. Kaitlyn picked up. It was Sven.

"How are you doin', hon?" she asked him.

"Sorry for calling so late. I just got home. I've been on the three to eleven shift all week, covering a co-worker on vacation." Sven let out a loud sigh. "I'll be so glad to get back to my own job next week."

"You don't sound happy."

"I've put my time in and pumping out sixty dinners in a half hour is pretty boring to me."

She laughed. "At least you're getting a work-out."

"You always look on the bright side. Anyway, the reason I was calling is to see if you're free to come to my place on Sunday, after lunch."

"Sure. What do you have in mind?"

"A leisurely jog in High Park. Then I'll make you dinner."

"Sounds great!"

After a long pause, he added, "Kaitlyn, I'm worried about you. You sound totally bushed. I'll let you get some rest. See you Sunday. Love you."

"Love you, " she replied right back.

Kaitlyn snoozed off, on the sofa, moments after the call.

Chapter Eighteen

Maxine completed her day and scanned the Toronto Star newspaper before leaving her office. One of the main headlines read *Corpse Identified as Wally Chipetta.*

Intrigued, Maxine went on to read the entire story. The police had discovered a man's body on January 18th – the day after Frank Jordan was murdered. Chipetta had been shot execution style, between the eyes. When police discovered the body, it had no identification and no fingerprints. The hands had been cut off. The identity of the man was achieved through comparision with dental records, a week later.

Maxine would ask Sergeant Fred O'Hallaran to look into a possible connection. She called him, but unfortunately, the Sergeant wasn't in, so she left him a voice-mail message.

If Wally Chippetta was the same man who was in Frank Jordan's apartment, then Holly would be in the clear. She'd done some digging of her own and through contacts she knew Wally's boss to be Marty Holstrom, who probably had him killed because he had failed to wipe out Holly too.

After gathering up her papers, Maxine headed out of the office and drove toward home. Now all Holly needed was an alibi. She had been in Waverley at the time of the murder, but Maxine needed to know if Holly had kept her bus ticket receipt. At least the receipt could partially establish that she was not in the city at the time of Wally's death. But first, she had to deal with the Stone case.

* * * *

Maxine read and re-read both the Crown screening report and the disclosure on the Stone case. It didn't look good for Becky. The Crown was looking for three years jail time for her part in the armed robbery.

It was absolutely ludicrous that anyone could believe that Becky could orchestrate anything. However, Becky's prior record didn't help her case at all and that, combined with her smooth arrest by the police in the get-away car were definitely not favourable toward her defense.

Maxine searched frantically for a legal loop-hole, but other than Becky's allegation that Harvey would shoot her for not participating, Maxine had nothing compelling to argue with.

Her client's only chance was to land a sympathetic Crown Attorney. Taylor hadn't been reassuring in his discussion of Ms. Kaitlyn Wolfe, leaving no doubt that Ms. Wolfe would be a well-prepared and formidable adversary. Maxine remembered the woman from Holly Nelson's bail court, but as yet, had no clue whatsoever about her subtleties and nuances.

Had Ms. Wolfe any particular social or political agenda? Did she negotiate well? Just how ambitious *was* this woman?

Maxine called up to the courthouse in Newmarket and set up a meeting with Ms. Wolfe for the following Friday. She must come up with a solid argument by then to debate. No doubt Becky would be doing a jail term – the issue was merely for how long.

Her thoughts turned to her life outside her law firm. Dr. Graham Barker, a cardiologist at Sunnybrook Hospital that shared his private practice in the same building, was taking her to a restaurant on the Danforth that evening. She hadn't seen Graham in over a week because their schedules hadn't permitted it. It would be a nice break. She was looking forward to seeing him again and hoping that this time around Graham wouldn't be paged to deal with an emergency surgery. On the flip side, she cancelled almost as many times as he did when she was stuck researching cases.

They took their own cars to the destination and met out in front of the bistro.

He walked up to her with a brilliant smile. "Hey, gorgeous."

"Hey back."

"Let's go eat, I'm wasting away to nothing." He chuckled.

* * * *

At the same time in Newmarket, Kaitlyn Wolfe stopped reading a complicated file only long enough to glance at the clock in her office. Well after seven, she would call it an evening. On her way home, Kaitlyn stopped by her favourite fast food restaurant for a take-out dinner. If Sven ever left her and the fast food restaurants closed, she would certainly starve to death.

Later that evening, Kaitlyn went for a lengthy run through the suburb where she lived. She ran over her usual two kilometers, and as she tried to fall asleep that night, she shed some pent-up tears from exhaustion.

Chapter Nineteen

"Rrrrr, Rodent, you made my toes tingle," Becky purred, between puffs from a joint.

"Thanks, babe. You're not so bad yourself." Rodent massaged her shoulder as he lay buck-naked on his bed. "Harvey doesn't know what he's missing."

"Yeah! Did you hear he's with some ditzy twerp named Mary-Jo?"

"I heard." Rodent took a drag on her joint. "The best part is that he has no idea that we set him up."

"I know, babe." She smiled an intelligent grin. "It was a stroke of luck to find that pile of crap car by the side of the road the day of the bank robbery. My little accident rendered the first car useless from the stink of garbage."

He passed back the smoke to her. "I couldn't believe our luck. It was almost worth having the crap beat out of me when I heard about our fortune."

"Speaking of fortune. I've got our take that I skimmed off Harv from the previous robberies, hidden."

"Once you've pled out your case, we'll be home free."

"Home free," she whispered coquettishly, instigating a second round of lovemaking.

Chapter Twenty

Kaitlyn spent part of Sunday helping Sven paint his apartment and then, as a diversion from both professional and domestic considerations, they went jogging on the paths in High Park. During a break, they talked a bit about the wedding with the appreciation that they were building a life and had a deep understanding that the wedding was only one day in the rest of their life together.

On her way in to work the following Monday morning, Kaitlyn bought a coffee and a muffin. She arrived at the courthouse fresh and ready to tackle another workweek. She leisured around, chatting up a couple of people before entering her office. She glanced at her diary. She had an appointment with Maxine Swayman that morning. She was thoroughly prepared for the meeting, having absorbed all the facts in the case, and she would not let this defense attorney intimidate her, despite her formidable reputation.

At promptly ten in the morning, Bridget, one of the administrative assistants, buzzed Kaitlyn by way of the intercom and announced that Maxine Swayman was here to see her. A strange little tremor in her belly overcame her as she rose to greet her visitor. Logic quelled her fears as she stood strong and proud, as was her custom. Kaitlyn walked to the reception area and greeted the tiny, well-manicured woman.

Maxine Swayman had the clearest creamy skin, dressed in a chic business. Dressed for success.

They shook hands. Ms. Swayman had a firm grip and showed no recognition of their first encounter, when Kaitlyn had been Stacey's victim of a cruel drug overdose.

"Can I call you Maxine?"

"Sure."

Kaitlyn lead the way to her office, and as she entered it, she became self-conscious of her surroundings, explaining, "I have most of my meetings over the telephone, so you'll have to excuse the mess."

"Relax. It looks like my office the first year I was called to the bar."

As was her custom, Kaitlyn remained stone-faced, trying to decide if Maxine Swayman was mocking her inexperience or making conversation.

"Let me move some files so you have a spot to write on." Kaitlyn hastily picked up a mishmash of file folders and binders, finding the pile a new resting place. "Do you want coffee, Maxine?"

"No thanks, I had one earlier."

She motioned Maxine to take a seat on the visitor's chair. The two exchanged pleasantries with an undercurrent of fact-finding about the other. Soon, the conversation turned to the business of the day.

"Becky Stone is a victim of circumstances in the commission of the crimes," Maxine began. Kaitlyn listened attentively. "She has a serious learning disability and made the wrong choice of becoming involved with Harvey Smith. Becky is beginning to thrive without Mr. Smith's influence and now has social workers helping her get a disability certificate. She is totally submissive, and her only motivator in the commission of this crime was her fear of Mr. Smith. This, of course, is not an admission of guilt, just pertinent history on my client."

"She has a record, and her involvement this time is substantial," said Kaitlyn firmly.

"What are you considering?"

"For the charges of dangerous operation of a

vehicle, operating a vehicle without a valid driver's license, theft of over five thousand dollars, possession of a firearm, and the conspiracy charge, I'm looking at five years."

"That's what is on your screening form, but had the robbery been successful, she would have not benefited from the proceeds of the crime, and I frankly don't understand the firearm charge."

"Upon the arrest, the police searched the car. A Beretta 9mm was found between Mr. Smith and Ms. Stone."

"Is that not the weapon that was seen in the bank's videotape?"

"Pardon me?" Kaitlyn asked, not seeing where this question was heading. Another Crown Attorney had prosecuted Harvey Smith. She'd briefly read the case file, but not in such detail as she should have. Come to think of it, the police report had mentioned a surveillance tape, but she hadn't requisitioned it for her review. She shook her head, disappointed at herself.

"In the police videotape, a disguised individual is carrying a small-calibre pistol and wearing the same clothes that Mr. Smith was wearing when he was arrested."

Kaitlyn maintained eye contact despite the knot growing in her stomach. Maxine had thoroughly researched the case as well.

"I wasn't told a videotape was recovered or the matching clothing?" This was not good at all.

"Also, I see you have listed the dangerous operation charge as indictable. Ms. Wolfe, no one was hurt; would you consider a summary conviction instead?"

"On what grounds?"

"It was such a minor accident and no one was injured. Becky didn't have the skills to drive and she was fearful for her life."

Kaitlyn reconsidered and nodded curtly. "The sentence will be custodial."

"Concerning the driving without a permit, Becky Stone may not have the cognitive retention to get a license, would you consider mischief instead?"

"For that one charge, I could."

"Would you consider dropping the weapon charge, changing the dangerous charge to summary, and giving her a concurrent sentence for the robbery and the mischief?"

"How much time are you proposing, Maxine?"

"Eighteen months, with twenty-four months probation afterwards."

"Twenty-four months and she serves at least six months for the robbery. A driving prohibition, weapon prohibition, three years probation and I'll convert the dangerous to a summary conviction."

Her opponent nodded, seeming satisfied. "I'll take it to my client."

"Oh. One more thing, she will undergo any counselling as deemed necessary by the professionals."

"That's probably best," Maxine agreed.

"You will get back to me?"

"Of course." Ms. Swayman rose. Kaitlyn took it as an indication that the meeting was over, but Ms. Swayman added, "Could we talk about another joint case?"

Kaitlyn gave her a nod, and Maxine sat back down again.

"You've got the wrong person in the Jordan murder."

With an exasperated demeanour, Kaitlyn said, "Oh! I suppose we've arrested the wrong person and, based on what you just said, I'll have her out by dinnertime."

"No, really. One of the real murderers, Wally Chipetta, was found dead, murdered. The police are trying to match the bullet recovered to the weapon that was used in the Jordan shooting."

"I'll hear how that turns out," Kaitlyn replied.

Maxine Swayman rose again and nodded curtly. "We'll talk again." She shook Kaitlyn's hand and headed out the door.

Kaitlyn glanced at the clock on the wall. Only twenty minutes after ten. The entire meeting had lasted less than half an hour. From her perspective, it hadn't gone at all well. An uncomfortable degree of professional humiliation crept through her. Terry Ouellette would support her decision in the Stone case, but she was embarrassed that she hadn't known about the surveillance video. In retrospect, she should have paid closer attention to details. She would be more thorough the next time.

There was a quality about Maxine Swayman that Kaitlyn respected, yet feared at the same time. Maxine had an air of affluence. The wealthy arrogance wasn't what Kaitlyn feared. Kaitlyn had not surrendered to Maxine, yet she had accepted a lower sentence than she had planned on prior to the meeting.

She could not reconcile her feelings, so she took a mid-morning break to walk around the park adjacent to the courthouse. It was rare for her to stop work and go outside in the middle of the morning.

The sun warmed the back of her neck. A falcon flew over the tops of the trees in search of prey. Her stomach started to settle. Kaitlyn's mind shifted back to her magical place from her childhood, meditating on its closeness to nature. In her ancestral culture, God and nature were one and the same. After ten minutes or so, she felt spiritually and physically revived.

She returned to her office and ploughed back into her work. Brenda Semple had stopped by during her absence, adding four more new case files to her pile. Kaitlyn read them over with enthusiasm.

Late in the afternoon, a thought struck her. Maxine Swayman offered a real challenge to Kaitlyn and to most Crown Attorneys. It was defense attorneys like Maxine that would compel Kaitlyn to become an even better prosecutor.

Bridget from the secretarial pool knocked on her door, entered, and placed a bouquet of gorgeous spring flowers on her desk. Kaitlyn reached for the card. The simple card stated, "I love you, *Mhiingan kwe*. Sven."

Kaitlyn showed Bridget the card. "Look, Sven is using my native name, which translated from Ojibway, means wolf woman.

"Isn't that special!" exclaimed Bridget. "That's sexy that he would pay that sort of attention to your First Nation's culture."

"You've got that right." Kaitlyn sighed aloud. "He's a catch."

"Yeah, the girls in the office practically drool over his good looks when he visits you. He could have been a movie star."

"You're so funny. My fiancée would be so embarrassed if he knew that you gals thought he was a looker. Anyway, I better get back to work."

"I'll put them in water for you, Kaitlyn."

"Thanks."

The flowers brightened the rest of her day with their intoxicating smell.

Chapter Twenty-One

"How'd you convince Harvey into committing a crime in Vaughan?" Rodent asked his girlfriend, Becky Stone, following another indoor workout.

"I gave him ssome crap about the get-away time being easier to manoeuvre in a small city instead of Toronto. He bought it and made the idea his own."

Rodent's lips curled into a sleazy grin. "How did you know about Harvey Smith's past encounter with the Crown?"

"Pillow talk, hon. He bragged that he shot an Indian cop when he was only seventeen. Anyway, this young Crown Attorney, an Indian woman named Kaitlyn Wolfe, tried a friend of mine in court. The last name rang a bell. I sensed a connection, so I read old newspapers at the library.

"That Wolfe Indian woman would have been about eleven or twelve when her dad died. She woulda' been just old enough to let Harv's crime screw up her life. Turns out she was the daughter of the cop. I just knew then that we'd have to get Harv in front of her somehow."

"Let him rot in jail for what he did to you."

"Let him rot in Hell for it." She left for the bathroom to run the shower.

Chapter Twenty-Two

Maxine called a meeting with Lauren McRay and Becky to discuss the offer made by the Crown Attorney. Lauren drove Becky to Maxine's office so she would not have to endure the horrors of the subway. As well, Lauren wanted to be available for emotional and general support.

The two women arrived at Maxine's office and were ushered in by her secretary. Becky Stone's skin looked even blotchier than Maxine remembered, and her eyes looked like two lumps of coal dropped in a snow bank.

"Sit, please," invited Maxine, gesturing toward two armchairs. "Coffee?"

"Please," said Lauren.

"Yup," added Becky.

Once everyone was settled in, Maxine began, "I met with the Crown Attorney, and we negotiated a deal that I believe is a fairly good one. The crown has agreed to twenty-four months in a jail for women. You will not be able to get a firearm permit for four years, and upon release, you will have to report to a probation officer for three years. Becky, you will also have to see a mental health professional and undergo whatever counselling the professional suggests."

"So, that's two years, right?"

"Yes, Becky, it is."

"I'll sstill be young enough and pretty enough so

men will still like me once I get out."

"Becky, do you understand that you will be going to jail for two years?" Lauren asked gently.

"They have TV in those places, don't they?"

"Yes, they do, as well as access to social workers and other professional services," Maxine added.

"Could she do better at trial?" Lauren asked Maxine.

"I doubt it. Too many variables could change at trial. Becky could get a tough judge, the Crown Attorney may be a different one, and with a jury, it can be unpredictable."

"So that's that. I'll get to watch my soaps and I won't have to glaze no doughnuts for two years. Tell 'em I'll take the deal."

Lauren and Maxine graciously ignored the gesture that accompanied the last statement Becky made. The woman was likely trying to imitate a character from television. Maxine sought eye contact with Becky. "The next time you come to court with Lauren, you will plead guilty, as you agreed. Do you understand?"

"Yup, guilty, guilty, guilty—"

"All right, Becky," Maxine said. "The Judge will ask you if you understand what you are pleading guilty to. Keep your answer short and honest."

Lauren interrupted: "Becky, I need you to confirm that you are okay with this. There will be no trial, and you will go to jail, maybe for two years."

Becky sighed. "I get it. It's a plea bargain, just like on television. The prossecutor will stand up and say what else I gotta' do along with the jail sentence."

Becky's watery eyes lost their focus and sparkled momentarily. "Then a bus will take me and the other girls, if there is any, to a jail somewheres in Ontario. Maybe the prossecutor will look like Alexis from my soap."

"Becky, Alexis is a made-up character, this is real life," Lauren berated her charge.

Maxine momentarily wondered how Becky could understand so much and then start babbling, on and on about soap operas.

"Becky? When the Judge asks you if you understand, what do you plan on saying?"

"I'll ssay that I did a bad thing. I drove a get-away car after a bank robbery. I'll ssay I'm ssorry and that I won't do it again. That'd be all." Becky turned to Lauren and tugged on her sleeve. "I want a hot dog. Ain't we done yet?"

Maxine gave Lauren a nod, confirming they were done. "Yes, Becky, we are. Lauren, please work with Becky on what she plans to say to the Judge. We'll see you here. Three weeks from today. Please excuse me, I've got to get back to court."

* * * *

Once Maxine met Holly Nelson in one of the conference rooms, she began with anticipation, "Holly, I have some important news. A man named Wally Chippeta was murdered the day after Frank's murder."

"Chippeta … I don't think I've ever heard of him."

"I believe that he may have been one of the shooters in Frank's murder. If so, it may be enough to get you off the hook."

"Oh, God. Oh, *please*, God," Holly wailed.

"Holly, this is very important. Did you find your bus ticket yet?"

"It would be in my wallet, the police still have it in lock-up."

"If you have the ticket stub to Waverley as well as the ticket stub back to Toronto, you have an established alibi during the time of Wally Chippeta's murder. This would be excellent news."

"The waitress from the restaurant might remember me." Holly looked at Maxine sheepishly. "I ordered and ate two breakfasts."

"It's possible. I mean, how many women would have two breakfasts?" Maxine said excitedly.

"Also, it is out of the tourist season, so she wouldn't have had too many new faces." Maxine nodded. "What if they ask me where I stayed the night Frank was murdered?"

"You will admit to the break and enter and hopefully they can dust the cottage for your prints. You run the risk of being convicted of the break and enter, but if it clears you of the murder, I advise you to confess."

"What am I looking at?"

"Because you felt you were running for your life, I believe you'll be convicted of the B & E only and will either get probation or, at worst, be forced to do minor jail-time. The Judge will convert it to time served, based on the time that you are doing now."

"Awesome."

"Hold on, Holly, we're not in the clear yet. I'll have to talk to Detective Sergeant O'Hallaran."

She sighed in dejection. "Let's hope he's nicer to you than he was to me."

"Not to worry. I'll let you know what happens," Maxine said as she whooshed out of the room.

* * * *

The next day, Maxine met with Detective Sergeant O'Hallaran. As he ushered her to his office, Maxine stared at the tall and stocky policeman's back, musing that he must have *some* common sense to make it to the Sergeant level.

He grunted and pointed at a chair. She sat down.

O'Hallaran sat on the corner of his desk. "How may I help you?"

Undaunted by his macho power and control tactic, she gave him a genuine smile. "Detective O'Hallaran, I'm about to save you time, money, and embarrassment. Does the name Wally Chippeta ring a bell?"

"Of course it does. Fifty-one division is handling the murder case." The 'why?' was plastered on his face.

"He was killed, execution style, the day after Frank Jordan. Check Mr. Jordan's known associates and you'll see the connection."

"Ms. Swayman, I'm a very busy man. Make your

point so I can go back to the business of catching the bad guys."

"Touché. If your lab would test the bullet from Frank Jordan's remains against the bullet from Chippeta's remains, you'd find that both projectiles came from the same small-calibre weapon."

"Oh, so now you're on the good side of the law, are you?"

She rose from her seat in her own power control move. "I don't have time for your pedantic games. Take me to your supervisor."

O'Hallaran paused; his stare assessing. "No need to be like that, I was just teasing you."

"Bullying is detestable, especially between professionals." She headed toward the door.

"*Please* ... let me hear what you have to say."

She spun around. "Once you have the report of the bullets matching in hand, you'll finally have to acknowledge that Holly Nelson is innocent. She was in Waverly, north of Barrie, when Chippeta was executed."

"Let me see some independent proof of this."

"You already have it." She couldn't suppress the grin that rose on her face. "Holly Nelson's bus receipt is locked up with her belongings, in your station. Oh, and I almost forgot; my client had a scrumptious breakfast of eggs, bacon, pancakes, and coffee in Waverly. She stuffed that receipt in her purse as well."

"Fine ... fine. I'll look into it."

* * * *

Detective Sergeant O'Hallaran ordered the lab technician to test the bullets from the two murders for comparison, as a courtesy to Maxine Swayman. More than anything, he wanted to avoid being cross-examined in court by this barracuda. Having to say that he didn't follow up on a possible lead could and might lead to professional embarrassment. She would crucify him under oath.

He further worked alongside the coroner to check

similarities between each bullet's point of entry and trajectory. Even if the two weapons didn't match, he knew the style of wound could show that the same man had committed the murder. A professional hitman would dispose of the weapon, not use the same gun in both murderers.

He also researched the Canadian Police Information Centre computer to investigate past criminal convictions of Wally Chippeta and Marty Holstrom. As per Holly's words, Marty Holstrom was the alleged ringleader. He was also the man per Holly Nelson who'd visited Frank Jordan the day prior to his demise to tell him to stop bringing attention to the organization. Holstrom was a known felon. The police already had him under investigation for a series of crimes.

It took O'Hallaran the better part of a day to sift through the arrest and conviction forms on the two men, so numerous were they. He didn't find a link between the two. However, he *did* discover that a third party named Les Reynolds had been convicted of assault along with Chippeta and had also been questioned in an assault charge involving Holstrom.

With these facts in mind, O'Hallaran began his plan of action. First, he sought a search warrant for Les Reynolds' place, then brought along Constable Randy Winters for support. Winters wasn't in the investigation branch of the police, but he was an exceptionally capable young man who he planned to eventually recruit for the branch.

By two in the afternoon, the team, including two crime technicians, Abe Johnston and Joe LaFountaine, drove up to Les Reynolds' abode, a dilapidated basement apartment in a duplex of a well-known drug area.

O'Hallaran told the technicians to wait in the cruiser, then he and Winters marched up to the premises. He knocked sharply on the door. After more insistent knocking, an unshaven, black-haired man answered.

"What the hell? Why are you waking me up?" Reynolds roared.

"Les Reynolds?"

"Uh-huh."

O'Hallaran grimaced as a gust of sour breath wafted through the doorway. Meanwhile, Les Reynolds sneered at Constable Winter's starched blue uniform and mandatory bullet-proof vest.

"Step aside," O'Hallaran ordered as he flashed his badge.

Reynolds stood his ground. "You got a warrant?"

"Do we need one?"

"I never let the police in without one."

"Well." O'Hallaran plucked the folded warrant from his vest's inside pocket. "We have one, signed by a judge, no less, allowing us to search your apartment."

Reynolds stood firm at this door. "No way, man. I'll tell you right now that a judge has no right violating my constitutional rights like this. I have a right not to incriminate myself."

"That doesn't apply in Canada," O'Hallaran reminded Reynolds. Shaking his head at Reynolds' delusion, he added, "You've been watching too much American TV. I love how you guys are such experts on your *rights.*" He waved Constable Winters inside. Reynolds could only gape and retreat at Winters' imposing bulk. O'Hallaran turned around and motioned the two technicians to come along.

The experienced technicians vacated the cruiser, and carrying their equipment, chatted as if this were a normal occurrence for them. Once Johnston's eyes were accustomed to the poor light of the dismal basement flat, he fished out a number of plastic bags to collect evidence in the living room while LaFountaine headed straight to Reynolds' bedroom.

Les Reynolds paced back and forth; sweat already pouring down from his forehead, which he sponged up with a clean towel. The more Reynolds paced, the more saturated his face became.

"Fred, Randy, you've got to see this," Johnston called. Both he and his partner rushed to Johnston's location. He was kneeling by an open garbage can.

"What was the address where the Frank Jordan murder took place?" Johnston asked.

"Grainger Tower. A high-rise condo building in Vaughan, in the penthouse. Why?"

Johnston smiled triumphantly and pulled out a fragment of paper from inside the can with the use of tweezers. "Well, here's a scrap paper that says, 'P2 Grainger Tower'."

O'Hallaran couldn't believe what they'd just uncovered. He patted Johnston on the shoulder. "Good job, my man."

A flash came from the bedroom. "Pay dirt!" LaFontaine's exuberant comment reverberated throughout the apartment.

Reynolds plopped onto the sofa, looking defeated. O'Hallaran ordered Winters to stand watch over Reynolds while he went to the bedroom to investigate. He negotiated the doorway, careful not to disturb any evidence. LaFountaine's camera now rested on the bed, and his gloved hand was reaching in a shoe box. He pulled out a Beretta 9mm by the silencer's end.

"I found the shoebox under a floorboard in this here closet." He secured the weapon and placed it into an evidence bag.

"Good work, Joe."

O'Hallaran returned to the living room, beaming. "Randy, read him his rights."

"Certainly." Constable Randy Winters succinctly recited the Miranda warning to a bewildered Reynolds.

* * * *

Daphne Hernandez, an employee in the Terminal 3 of the Toronto International Airport, loved her spy movies and the intricacies of being a spy. As a coffee hostess, she worked the early morning shift so she could have her afternoons free for her soap operas.

She had an amazing capacity for remembering even the tiniest detail about people. When harried or arrogant businessmen barely acknowledged her, she fantasized on their status. Perhaps they were international business owners focusing on vital worldwide problems instead of paying basic human contact to her.

It was a frigid, cold day in January when Daphne served a dark-haired man of about fifty. The man's indigo blue suit with gray-hued accented stripes caught her notice. To Daphne's logic, the scuffed brown penny loafers spelled inconsistency. Why was this tall man wearing shoes that clashed with his outfit?

Initially, her fantasy settled on a bachelor without a partner to advise him how to dress. Next, she revised her scenario to an overworked accountant who had met with a client on the way to the airport for his annual vacation with his family. But then, the mystery man wore no wedding ring.

When the mystery man reached for his coffee, Daphne's astuteness caught the personalized cuff links with the initials M. H. Yes, she smiled inwardly; she liked the overworked accountant theory who was deviating from his usual meticulous appearance. She was sure of her theory when the would-be accountant marched toward the departure's lounge of the Cayman Islands' flights.

Another mystery solved. Oh, what fun!

* * * *

"Rodent, will you wait fur me?"

He looked at his lover, Becky, a might confused. "Wait for you ... for what?"

"Come on now, you know that I'm going to the chick country club for twenty-four months, but with good behaviour, I'll be out in eighteen monthss."

"Oh that ... of *course* I'll wait," said Rodent with heavy sincerity.

Becky massaged his shoulders, relieved to hear Rodent confirm what she assumed. "Of course you will. I've got the money stashed. I'll give you enough to get by until I get out, though. You want to hear something funny?"

"Sure. Go on."

"Lauren, my social worker, fast-tracked me, so once I'm released, our government will give me about a grand a month," she slowed her speech down and giggled. "Because of my learning disability."

Rodent grinned. "That's priceless! How'd you pull off the stupid act for so long?"

"It was easy, really. I'm dyslexic. I have trouble reading. That part isn't a lie. I mimicked a dumb character from a TV show for the rest of it. I even fooled the social worker! Cash for life disability cheques .... Won my very own lotto!"

He fondled her breasts. "I'm going to miss those while you're in jail."

Chapter Twenty-Three

Detective O'Hallaran requested the presence of Holly Nelson. Without her legal council present, she looked at him fearfully as he loomed over her.

"Ms. Nelson, we have arrested the man responsible for Frank's murder."

She exhaled heavily in relief and began to shake uncontrollably. "Who is he?"

"Les Reynolds. A man with a lengthy criminal record. We questioned him thoroughly, but he won't implicate anyone else."

"So, I am not safe." Holly gazed into space, fighting tears.

"I don't believe so."

At his reply, she returned her attention to him. "What are my options?"

"You can remain incarcerated, for your protection, as a material witness, or we can hide you in a shelter for abused women, although there is the possibility shelter staff may not take you because your presence may endanger the other residents."

"Then I'll stay here," she said firmly.

"So be it."

* * * *

Terry Ouellette beamed. "Kaitlyn, have a seat." He

pulled out a velvet-backed chair at Bistro Estelle, the most lavish restaurant in Vaughan.

The waiter appeared and filled their crystal water goblets. He placed the damask napkin on Kaitlyn's lap and offered, "May I get you a beverage?"

She smiled. "Water is fine, thank you."

"Sir?"

"Coffee."

"Thank you, sir. Do you need a few minutes to read the menu?"

Terry nodded to the waiter who then bowed away.

"Kaitlyn, I've asked you to lunch today to talk."

She pursed her lips together and settled in to listen.

"Because of your quick thinking, the police have a murderer in custody for both the Frank Jordan murder and the Wally Chippeta murder. I'm proud to be working with you."

She nodded, unable to answer with words.

"There is also a possibility that your work may lead to the arrest of Marty Holstrom. The major crimes squad have devoted literally thousands of hours trying to capture this suspected mobster, and your witness may be able to link him into putting out a hit on both Jordan and Chippeta. This is great work."

Terry picked up his menu, and taking her cue from him, Kaitlyn did likewise. Quickly, they made their own choice and replaced the menus on the table. The waiter reappeared, and they ordered. Terry ordered chicken Neptune – a chicken breast stuffed with crab meat smothered in a creamy ginger sauce – while she selected a salmon fillet topped with a buttery dill sauce.

"Anyway, you're probably curious why I asked you to lunch."

"Yes, I am very curious."

"I've never had a first-year Assistant Crown Attorney try a double murder case before, but because of your enormous skills and tenacity, I'd like for you to try the killer of Jordan and Chippeta."

"Les Reynolds?"

"Exactly. Les Reynolds." He paused, taking a sip of

his coffee. "It's a huge case. The newscasts will be covering that one from opening to closing comments. If it feels at all overwhelming, I'll have Trevor Knight act as second chair."

Kaitlyn steeled herself and achieved her usual calm exterior, but inside she was completely shaky. It would be a tremendous amount of work to prepare for a double murder case. As well, the accused's lengthy record would likely have him hire an intimidating defense team.

Terry's testing me. "I'd be glad to try Les Reynolds, but I won't need a second chair. I may talk over the trial strategy with either Trevor or you but ...." She breathed in deeply. "I'm ready for it. As a matter of fact, I know more about the case than anyone else."

Her supervisor visibly relaxed. "That's the kind of confidence I need to see. The case is yours."

She smiled her thanks then looked forward to her first bite as the waiter placed her plate before her.

She swallowed a forkful of her lunch. "Hummmm, this salmon is to die for, Terry."

"My chicken is also great." He forked another chunk of chicken. "Get used to this restaurant, it's where all the lawyers and judges eat while they're in Vaughan."

"I can see why." She sobered. "I do have a big concern about the Reynolds trial."

"Your key witness?" he asked in response to her statement.

"I have grave concerns about Holly Nelson's safety."

Terry laid his fork down and dabbed at his lips with his napkin. "Not to worry. Holly is currently in protective custody until the trial. After the trial, I'll personally negotiate a place for her in the Witness Relocation Program."

"She's just a kid, Terry. Is witness relocation such a good idea?"

He shrugged. "I'm out of options. She chose the life, and to keep her alive, we have a moral obligation to keep her safe."

She agreed through a curt nod. "I hope she's

mature enough to stay hidden."

"I don't know the woman, but witnessing her boyfriend being gunned down may have matured her more than we'll ever know."

"You're probably right …. She's so young."

"It's better to be young and living under a new identity than laying on a slab, dead."

"Good point."

He picked up his fork, paused, then added, "It's normal for you to have concerns about the witness."

Kaitlyn sighed. "I just feel so sad for her."

He pointed the fork at her. "Don't lose that quality. Our court could use more Crown Attorneys who have empathy."

After sharing lunch with Terry, Kaitlyn got a message to visit Holly through the protective custody officials, wanting to set up a victim interview. The reply stated that Holly wanted to speak to her lawyer before she consented to a meeting, but otherwise she was keen on explaining the connection between Marty Holstrom and Frank Jordan.

* * * *

The next day, Maxine and Holly arrived at Kaitlyn's cluttered office, a small windowless room within the Newmarket Court.

"I have read the statement you gave to the police," the Crown Attorney addressed Holly, "but I would also like you to tell me all of the details you can remember about the day your boyfriend was shot."

Holly recounted the story to Ms. Wolfe in detail. She eloquently explained that it had, after all, been a night to remember – her personal version of the day John F. Kennedy was murdered, in which *everybody* remembers *everything*. She was heartbroken as she described finding her boyfriend dead.

Obviously, this woman hadn't killed Frank Jordan. Genuine tears of grief streamed down her client's face. How could a homicide detective not see the love and sadness in her eyes? Maybe it took a woman to understand her loss.

Maxine clarified, "The two days after the murder, my client's whereabouts can be verified. Seeking escape, Holly jumped aboard the first bus out of town. Holly can provide receipts. She hid out in a hick town, planning a strategy, then she returned to the city. Her fleeing was a foolish and careless move, but in the wake of such trauma, who could blame her?"

Maxine provided details about the location where Holly held up for forty-eight hours. Ms. Wolfe didn't quiz them further.

"Ms. Nelson, please tell me every detail about the conversation you overheard between Frank and Marty Holstrom," Kaitlyn prodded.

Holly nodded. "I had been lounging in the bedroom when the doorbell rang. Frank answered it and I heard him in his schmoozing voice offer the visitor a coffee. But the man flatly refused coffee or any hospitality. Frank then said, 'Marty, my man. What can I do for you today?'

"There was a silence then the visitor barked, 'Knock off the flashy lifestyle, asshole. It's bad for business, it makes you look too conspicuous. Your partying ways will bring down the whole organization. Clean up your act, or there'll be consequences. *Real bad consequences.*' Frank replied, 'Yeah, yeah, I get it.' "

The Crown Attorney stopped writing notes and looked directly at Ms. Nelson. "You are sure that your boyfriend used the name Marty?" Holly confirmed with a nod. "What happened next?" Kaitlyn enquired.

"I heard his warning to Frank. Then I hear Marty say 'I'm glad we've reached an understanding.' Then the apartment door slammed shut."

"Would you recognize this man's voice?" The crown asked.

"I can even point him out to you."

"But you said you were in the bedroom?"

Holly reddened. "I'm a curious individual. I opened the door a crack to see who Frank was talking to. It was Marty Holstrom, all right."

"Did Frank mind the warning?"

She bit her lip and shook her head. "He ordered a limo for that very evening. We never go anywhere on Tuesdays, but he just ordered a ride just the same."

Chapter Twenty-Four

On the court date, Les Reynolds pled not guilty to the murders of Frank Jordan and Wally Chippeta. He lacked an alibi; however, he had nothing to lose by going to trial.

The defense had elected to have the case heard only by a judge and not both judge and jury. Kaitlyn knew of this defense strategy; minimize the stigma of representing a killer for hire. The defense attorney, Harry Metzcer, certainly didn't want a number of retired suburban homeowners decide the future of his client.

Metzcer stood by the enclosed prisoner's area where Les Reynolds stood in an ill-fitting polyester suit. Reynolds sneered at Kaitlyn as she put out her materials for the case.

From the corner of her eye, she noticed Metzcer whispering to his client followed by a bout of laughter from both men.

She shook her head at their malice. What a ridiculous stunt. She mentally blocked them out, bent on not having those men break her confidence.

Court was called to order. Kaitlyn stood to give her opening statement. "Your Honour, Lester Reynolds is a killer for hire who murdered two of his business acquaintances. A merciless and sadistic man who enjoys inflicting pain on others. If the court does not stop him this time, he will only maim and kill others in the future.

"The prosecution has a witness who will identify Mr. Reynolds' voice at the scene of the Jordan murder. We also have a number of forensic links to the crime scenes. We will prove that Mr. Reynolds committed both homicides. Thank you, Your Honour." She seated herself.

Next, Mr. Metzcer was called to provide his opening address. "Your Honour, my client may have known both of the deceased men. However, the prosecution has taken a loose association and turned it into a *'made-for-television'* drama. Mr. Reynolds had the unfortunate luck of shooting billiards with both of the victims, on occasion. He is a house painter by trade who suffers from extreme alcoholism. Mr. Reynolds doesn't have the capacity at this time to participate in his vocation, let alone be part of anyone else's business.

"The defense will discount each piece of the Crown's evidence and prove that, as a chronic alcoholic, Mr. Reynolds is simply not physically fit enough to commit the crimes which he is charged with. Thank you, Your Honour."

Kaitlyn began the case by calling a forensics' expert named Abe Johnston to the stand. Mr. Johnston was sworn in.

"What is your occupation, Mr. Johnston?" she began her questioning.

"I am a crime scene investigator for the Centre for Forensic Sciences in Toronto." He looked at the judge. "However, I was recently seconded to the police force in Newmarket to manage the forensic science department."

Kaitlyn moved forward with her line of questions, "Would you tell us about your relevant credentials."

"I have an undergraduate science degree from the University of Toronto, a Masters of Science in Forensic Science Degree from George Washington University – District of Columbia, and I'm an associate professor at the University of Toronto."

"Clearly you are well qualified in the field of forensic science."

Johnston kept his attention on Kaitlyn and said, "I would have to agree."

"Mr. Johnston, tell this court how you are involved in this case."

The witness cleared his throat. "I was the lead investigator in the execution of the search warrant of Mr. Reynolds' apartment."

"Were you the only technician present?"

"I had a colleague, Mr. Joseph LaFountaine, with me. Once Mr. Reynolds was showed the search warrant, we began our investigation."

"Please tell us what you found on the premises."

"I found a scrap of paper with the words 'P2 Grainger Tower' written on it."

"And what is this scrap paper linking to?" Kaitlyn asked.

"That is the address of the condominium which Holly Nelson and Frank Jordan shared."

"Please, go on."

"I carefully stored the paper in a numbered plastic bag and stowed the evidence in my investigation briefcase."

Kaitlyn turned to the witness on the stand. "Did you run any tests on the paper?"

"Back at the crime lab, I dusted the paper for fingerprints."

"What were the results?"

"Fingerprints lifted matched those of Wally Chippeta on the computer database."

"You mean the same Wally Chippeta who was brutally murdered?"

Harry Metzcer jumped to his feet: "Objection, Ms. Wolfe is testifying."

"Rephrase, Your Honour?" She paced across the courtroom. "Please confirm how you know those fingerprints belonged to Wally Chippeta."

"Both a thumb and an index print were lifted from the paper. These prints provided a seven-point match to the fingerprints that we had on file for Mr. Chippeta."

"Seven-point match, is that a good reliable match?"

"Yes, Ms. Wolfe, both prints are a superb match to Mr. Chippeta."

"Since you were the supervising technician on site, please tell us what your colleague Mr. LaFountaine discovered."

He looked accusingly toward the defense table. "A tiny Beretta 9mm handgun."

Kaitlyn heard the reactive gasp from an onlooker behind her.

She took this moment to reach for a photograph in a plastic sleeve. "Your Honour, I'd like to have this photograph entered as exhibit four."

"So noted."

"Mr. Johnston, please tell the judge what this is a picture of."

"It's the photograph my partner took at the scene where he found the Beretta 9mm handgun with silencer attached inside a shoe box collected from beneath floorboards inside the bedroom closet."

"Beneath floorboards?"

"Yes, madam. A sure sign he was trying to hide it."

Kaitlyn walked the photo to the judge. "Please take a good look at this gun. It's tiny but deadly." She turned to her witness. "When you tested this lethal firearm, what did you learn?"

"Objection."

"What are you objecting to, Mr. Metzcer?" asked the Judge.

"I'm objecting to the word lethal."

"Guns kill people, Mr. Metzer," The Judge reminded the defense. "Ms. Wolfe, please continue."

"What did you learn from this weapon while you tested it?"

Mr. Johnston, a seasoned witness, paused, then spoke up, "It's the weapon that was used to murder both Frank Jordan and Wally Chippeta. Projectile comparison matched those recovered from both murders."

"Anything else you learned from that weapon?"

"Both the *lethal* Beretta handgun and the bullets have Mr. Reynolds' fingerprints on them."

More gasps rose from the gallery.

"Thank you, Mr. Johnston. I have no further questions at this time."

Mr. Metzcer tried to discredit her witness, without success, the science of forensics being specific enough. She knew that Mr. Johnston's testimony was accepted as accurate.

* * * *

Following the expert's testimony, court broke for lunch. Metzcer met with his client in a small conference area beside the courtroom to strategize.

"You told me that the prosecutor was an inexperienced girl!" growled Reynolds. "She's smart. She knows her stuff. That judge is going to send me away for sure."

Metzcer planted a serious look on his client. "Look, Les, a lot will depend on Holly Nelson's testimony. From what you told me, she's a party girl. Probably not too bright a girl. I'll discredit her and enjoy the process." He shook his head in worry. "Forensics definitely hurts our case, but I believe I can make the next witness appear stupid, unreliable."

"Look, man, you better."

Les's threatening tone not could be missed and Metzer felt a pressure build in his chest.

Reynolds added with worried look, "That Crown, she's killin' me." Sweat ran uncontrollably from his forehead, and he tried to slow its progress with a tissue. To Metzcer, Les Reynolds looked like a beaten old man.

"Les, have you considered letting me plea the case out?"

"Let's see if you can defeat the girlfriend first, and if not, then go to the Crown, *please*."

"Done."

Harry Metzcer concluded his meeting with his client and hurried to a nearby sandwich shop. He wolfed down a tomato on rye bread sandwich while considering his case. Les Reynolds was unravelling; this would not help

215

matters any.

* * * *

Court reconvened and Holly Nelson was called to the stand. The court officer fetched her from the witness area. As she was guided into the courtroom, Metzer's spirits fell.

As if to belie any suggestion that she was a party girl, Holly had come to court dressed in a white lace blouse with a lengthy black skirt. The effect was that of an ever-so-very-proper secretary. Metzcer sweated profusely as though his insides went into knots, wringing out the sweat.

The court services officer swore the new witness in. Holly confirmed her address as being the penthouse which she shared with Frank. Her calm appearance and her clear eyes frazzled Harry Metzcer even more. She had not partied the night before.

Confidently rising from her chair, the Crown approached the witness. "Tell me, Holly, where were you at the time of your boyfriend's execution?"

"Objection! I strenuously object to the term execution." The word 'executed' projected his client as a gangster.

"Sustained," the Judge ordered.

"I'll rephrase, Your Honour. When your boyfriend was gunned down, where were you, Ms. Nelson?"

"In our bedroom, picking out an outfit to wear for the evening's outing. I closed the door when I heard people in the apartment." Holly Nelson spoke in a demure voice and she unwaveringly chose her words.

"Why close the door, were you half dressed?" Kaitlyn asked next.

"No. Habit."

"What do you mean by 'habit'?"

"Frank and I had an agreement. I wouldn't listen to his business discussions or try to find out who any of his business friends were."

"Why was that?"

"My boyfriend claimed that the less I knew, the better. He may have made his money in a less than traditional way, but he was a gentleman who wanted to protect me from harm." Holly's voice shook and her lower lip trembled, as good memories seemed to come back to her.

"Please describe for the court what happened next."

"Frank told me time and time again that if there were trouble, I should hide in what he called the 'panic place.' "

"Panic place?"

Holly waved her hand as if minimizing the term. "It's a tiny room with a false wall about a foot and a half out from the real wall in our bedroom. Frank built it himself. It was a storage place for, uh ...."

"For storing what, Ms. Nelson?"

"Um, money. The door was actually a dresser that swung open and then could be locked from the inside."

"Who did the shooter sound like?"

"Objection. Your Honour, the witness was in an enclosed space and, in any event, is not an expert in voice recognition."

"Overruled. The witness is instructed to answer."

"Frank had the stereo on with loud classical music, so the shooter raised his voice and ended up yelling. That man was Les Reynolds. Frank and I had run into Les at a dance club back in October of last year and had spent the entire night talking to one another, so I got to know his voice pretty well," responded Holly with assurance.

"Do you believe that is how the shooter knew that your boyfriend had a life partner?"

"Yes, I do."

"Let's backtrack, Ms. Nelson. Why did you hide?"

"As I said, those were Frank's instructions." Holly broke into great, hiccupping sobs. "I knew that I would be next if I didn't, and there was nothing I could do anyway; I have to live the rest of my life, knowing I abandoned Frank ...."

"Sorry, I have to keep up with the questions ... a

tissue for the witness, please?" The court officer obliged. "What made you think ... well, of course, they couldn't afford the risk of a witness ...."

"I heard Mr. Reynolds say to the other man, 'if we find the bitch' ... that was me ... they'd do me in too."

"If it makes you feel any better, I don't see that you could have acted otherwise. No other questions of this witness."

Harry Metzcer stood and smiled at the Judge then at the witness. "Ms. Nelson, what was your physical condition at the time of the shooting?"

"I don't understand the question."

"Were you high on drugs or alcohol?" he asked with a trace of sarcasm.

Kaitlyn jumped to her feet and practically shouted, "Objection. Leading."

"Sustained," the Judge replied.

"I'll rephrase. Do you take drugs and alcohol on a regular basis?"

"Yes, but in very small quantities," Holly admitted. "I'll have about four drinks in a night and the occasional marijuana cigarette. I am not addicted at all, if that's what you are implying."

"On the day in question, had you been drinking or taking drugs?"

"No. Frank had smoked up our marijuana stash that day. I was clean and sober."

Metzcer seemed surprised at the sincere way Holly Nelson answered his question. He felt another line of questioning would be best. "How thick was the door to this, uh, panic place?"

"The thickness of a chest of drawers."

"And what was in the chest of drawers?"

"Clothes ... underwear ... um, lingerie ...."

"How could you possibly hear through all that?"

"The drywall either side of the dresser was a half-inch thick, Frank had said. It acted like a sounding board. Even with the music, I could pretty well overhear everything."

Frustrated by Holly's reserve, Metzcer changed his

angle again. "What is your occupation?"

"I guess you would have to say that I am, or was, a housewife. I took care of Frank's apartment and prepared his meals."

Metzcer could see he was not getting very far on his cross-examination, yet he persevered. "Why did you run after the event?"

"I heard Les Reynolds say the boss would put a hit out on me. I was terrified! I had to get away to stay alive."

"Ms. Nelson, we have not established that the man in the apartment was Les Reynolds."

Holly looked Metzcer straight in the eye. "In my mind, I certainly have."

"No further questions of this witness, Your Honour, but I would like to exercise my right to recall the witness at a later time."

"So noted," the judge answered.

Chapter Twenty-Five

After the cross-examination of Holly Nelson, the court adjourned for the afternoon break and Harry Metzcer sought Les Reynolds, held within the prisoner's area of the court.

Upon seeing him enter the area, Les began in a hushed but frantic tone, "That bitch is not so stupid after all."

Harry lifted his hands in a helpless gesture. "Les, I am as surprised as you are. I figured she would be some drug-addicted party girl. Wolfe has converted her into a credible witness."

"We've got a bigger problem."

"What's that?" the lawyer asked.

"Marty up and skipped the country. Metzcer, it's all going to fall on my head!"

"Are you sure about Marty?"

Les slumped onto the prisoner bench and wiped his face in a defeated gesture. "Yeah. Real positive. One of my buddies in the joint told me that Marty just took a flight to the Cayman Islands."

"Oh, brother." Metzcer slumped beside the prisoner, "Do the cops know?"

"Don't see how they could."

"I'll talk to the prosecutor about a deal, then."

"Yeah, but remember, I don't roll over on Marty. If I ever implicated him, he'd eventually come back and kill me."

"We will make that a condition. Don't let on that Marty is gone, though."

"Got it." Les wiped his forehead and straightened in hope.

"I'll ask the Crown for an appointment."

Les nodded vigorously. "Sounds like a plan."

* * * *

Kaitlyn glanced at her watch. The fifteen-minute break was nearly over. The Court Services Officer would be opening the court soon. She hurried back and was about to open the courtroom door when she felt a hand on her shoulder. She spun around about to give the person a piece of her mind.

A bleary eyed Harry Metzcer was perspiring like a marathon runner.

"Yes?"

"Ms. Wolfe, can I have a quick word in the law library?"

"Very well, but we don't have long."

"I know."

Once seated in the library, he went right to the point. "My client is willing to change his plea, provided you are lenient on him at the sentencing hearing."

"Why would I want to accept a plea now?"

Harry averted his eyes. "Mr. Reynolds just wants to own up to his part in the Jordan murder and accept his sentence."

"What about the Chippeta murder?"

"He'll plead to that as well."

Kaitlyn was a tad confused. "On the Crown Screening form I had asked for life imprisonment."

"Twenty-five years?"

"As you well know, Mr. Metzcer, first degree murder has a minimum punishment of twenty-five years when it is an intentional killing. Your client committed two murders."

Metzcer continued to sweat. "Twenty-five concurrent?"

"Consecutive with no eligibility of parole until he's served at least twenty years."

"Ms. Wolfe, you're young and eager. I get that. But please be reasonable."

She rose from the table and headed to the door.

"Wait, wait, I'll talk to my client."

Kaitlyn looked over her shoulder. "Fine," she said as she maintained her well-rehearsed non-emotional stare.

Back in the courtroom, she witnessed Metzcer whispering the deal to the defendant. Reynolds nodded his head. Metzcer then rose and came to her.

"You drive a hard bargain, but my client is accepting the plea."

The two lawyers requested an approach to the Judge who waved them close. Both explained that they had come to an agreement. The Judge nodded and both counsels returned to their table. Judge Stewart ordered Les Reynolds to stand and formally change his plea to guilty.

Judge Stewart sent him away to prison, pending a sentencing hearing in three weeks time.

As the court officers took Les Reynolds away, he looked hopelessly downtrodden and pissed off.

Chapter Twenty-Six

"It's over," Holly whispered to herself, feeling a heavy weight lifted from her shoulders. "I'm free."

Once court was adjourned for the day, Ms. Wolfe asked to see Holly. Together, they drove back to her office, and once they were seated, her lawyer said, "You did wonderfully today, Holly, just great."

"Thank you, Ms. Wolfe." Those were the only words that Holly could manage as she was still chock full of feelings.

"I didn't expect it to end as quickly as it did; however, I am happy with the results," Ms. Wolfe said kindly. "I wanted to meet with you again and discuss with you the Witness Relocation Program."

Holly must have still had a blank look on her face as Ms. Wolfe asked, "Are you still interested in it?"

Holly averted her eyes briefly to think on it then returned her attention to Ms. Wolfe with her answer. "I think so. My adoptive parents are nice, but, other than them, I really don't have anyone. My sisters didn't want too much to do with me after I moved in with Frank."

"That's such a shame, Holly."

"Yeah." Holly sighed wistfully. "I don't think I'll be missed."

"Have you ever thought about what you'd want to do with your life?"

"I'd like to get a college diploma in graphic arts.

When I set my mind to it, I can be really creative. I figure if I'm taught how to use a computer, I could design some pretty neat stuff. There's so much in the way of logo design now, in clothing and that sort of thing."

"That sounds like a reasonable and constructive goal. It'll work in your favour if you have a plan. I can probably get someone from the Department of Justice to set you up in a city that has a good graphics program. Until you are established in your field, they can provide you with funds to help you. How does that sound?"

Holly's spirits brightened. "Really? Wow!" Then feeling there might be a catch, she sobered. "What are the conditions?"

"If the police ever catch Marty Holstrom, you will be expected to come back to testify."

"Wait, what do you mean *if* you ever catch him?"

"He's skipped his apartment. We don't know where he's gone."

A moment of panic seized her. "So, I really am not safe as Holly Nelson, am I, Ms. Wolfe?"

"Not any more."

Chapter Twenty-Seven

On the appointed day, Lauren McRay, Becky Stone's social worker, ushered the frightened woman into the courtroom. In a floral dress donated to her at the homeless shelter, Becky seemed to all as overwhelmed by the somber majesty of the court.

However, Becky quickly spied her ex, Harvey Smith, seated at the back of the courtroom and accompanied by Mary-Jo. Becky pointed a crooked finger at him for Lauren's benefit.

* * * *

"Harvey Smith is called to the stand," the court clerk called.

Once Mr. Smith was introduced and sworn in, Kaitlyn grabbed the file, a red one from the case files, and opened it. "Mr. Smith has been a career criminal for at least the last eighteen years, fact supported by arrests and or complaints on record. I reject the pleadings of the parole officer and feel it is in society's best interest to incarcerate Harvey Smith for a minimum of twelve years."

"Shit! Spyke, do something. That Crown Attorney's going for my balls."

Kaitlyn overheard his hoarse whispered plead to his defense attorney. The rude comment did not escape the

Judge's ears either; he looked as if about to say something, then thought better of it and let the matter go.

Vern Spyke, defense lawyer for Harvey, spoke up. "Your Honour, Mr. Smith pled guilty to his minor role in the robbery and the Crown already accepted his plea pending the sentencing recommendation of the parole office."

"I can hear you, Mr. Spyke, and while I'm at it, you will admonish your client and warn him to watch his mouth in my court." The icy tone of Justice Grainge from the bench let on that another outburst would bring forth consequences.

"Er, sorry, Your Honour."

"Your Honour, I'd like to present Mr. Smith's arrest sheet." Kaitlyn passed the document to the bailiff, who handed it to the Judge. "His bad streak began at age sixteen. He shot a co-defendant in the foot. At eighteen, he shot a convenience store clerk and was incarcerated for six years for this crime. Evidently, Mr. Smith learned nothing during those years of incarceration since, upon his release, he did more robberies, culminating with the one he's plead guilty to. Mr. Smith is a dangerous man. For the safety of society, he needs to be in jail for as many years as the law permits for this crime."

Justice Grainge read the report then raised a sombre glance to Kaitlyn. "I agree with you, Ms. Wolfe. Harvey Smith, you will rise." Mr. Smith did as instructed. "You are sentenced to twelve years of incarceration for your role in the armed robbery."

As Mr. Smith was lead away in handcuffs, he glanced back over his shoulder and met Becky Stone's stare. Kaitlyn captured the smirk on Becky's face.

The Judge called a recess after the Smith verdict. Kaitlyn rushed out of the courtroom, making eye contact with Becky Stone. For the first time, Kaitlyn noted the expression of a fighter in those eyes.

* * * *

Kaitlyn had a moral obligation to disclose her conflict of

interest, but was emotionally unable to let anyone else handle the sentencing of Harvey Smith.

She had to avenge her dad's death.

She sat on the bench outside the courthouse, clenching and unclenching her fists. She'd known for about a month that Harvey was her father's killer. A typed, unsigned letter in her mailbox stated Harvey Smith to be the shooter in her dad's demise. Then she'd read of his prior convictions, and how he'd committed crimes with James Booth, the man who'd done time for killing her father. When she reread Harvey's conviction sheet, she'd noted that he'd been arrested as a co-defendant with James Booth on another robbery. In her heart, she was certain of Harvey Smith's role in the death of her father.

Her father's murderer would finally be punished for Clarence's death.

A thought came to her. Did that slow Becky Stone know anything? From their last eye contact, Kaitlyn wondered if she'd been played. If Becky disclosed the connection, she could be disbarred. She couldn't contemplate on her life then. Kaitlyn gave herself a mental shake. She must have misinterpreted the look she saw on Becky's face. It's a good thing that Becky was too slow to know *anything*.

* * * *

Becky and Lauren waited for over two hours until the court officer called Becky's name. The woman clumsily rose and came to stand at the front of the courtroom where Maxine Swayman stood. Becky looked nervous and frightened by the Judge in his sombre black robes. She was asked to enter a plea.

She simply stated: "Guilty."

Kaitlyn offered the conditions of the plea arrangement with the confidence and composure that had already made her something of a legend in the local legal community.

"Ms. Stone, " Justice Grainge said in a gruff voice.

Kaitlyn held her breath, seeing Becky's shaking hands and wobbly posture. "Do you understand what Ms. Wolfe has just proposed?

"Yeah, yeah I do."

"Explain it to me, please."

"I'll go to jail for about tttwo years for doin' a really bad thing."

"Yes, Ms. Stone, and explain to the court, for the record what you did."

"Well, uh, um, it's like ...."

"Ms. Stone, the recorder has to put this in the transcript, please speak up."

Becky stood a little taller, glanced demurely at Lauren, and stated, "I met a bad, bad, man and he made me drive a get-away car in an armed robbery. I didn' do a good job of driving and the car got all smashed up by me hittin' some garbage.

"I did a bad, bad, thing and now I gotss to go to jail and I also gotss to meet with a pssychol ... I can't say the word, like a worker to teach me how to not do bad stuff ever agin."

"Ms. Stone, I sincerely hope that you use your time in prison well by receiving the counselling that you need." The Judge went on to declare, "I accept the sentencing recommendation as read."

The court officer ushered Becky Stone out of the courtroom to a holding area. She shot a weak glance back at Lauren and Maxine on her way out, fear and apprehension showing in her eyes.

The next case was called and Kaitlyn carried on in her official capacity.

Maxine Swayman paused to say good-bye to the Outreach Worker and then was off at her usual brisk pace out the door and on to her next case.

* * * *

Becky Stone sat patiently in a ten-foot by ten-foot cell for the next six hours. It wouldn't do to start her time in jail with a poor outlook. At five in the evening, she was transported in a prison van to be housed in a Toronto jail for women. She'd been told that within the month, she would be transferred to a jail in the country for the duration of her sentence. Her first night was so noisy and busy that she could barely hear the television over the din of sixty, mostly hostile, strangers.

Hopefully, the next jail would be better.

Chapter Twenty-Eight

A willowy dark-haired woman, carrying a leather portfolio containing two years' worth of college level design projects, strode confidently down the street to the somewhat eclectic offices of The Art Agency of British Columbia, a small ostentatiously-named advertising agency in North Vancouver. Larry McDermott, the proprietor of the agency, met the woman at the front desk and invited her into his office.

After assessing the young designer's creations for twenty minutes, he said, "Lacie Marsdon, if you are willing to spend a portion of your time designing and some of your time assisting the others in the creative department, then I would like to hire you."

"Thank you, sir. I would." Holly Nelson, now known as Lacie Marsdon, was finally making her own way, safe.

Chapter Twenty-Nine

"Don't you feel like a run?" Sven asked Kaitlyn as he tied his jogging shoes.

Kaitlyn slid on an extra sweater. "Normally, I'd like a run, but for this time could we just take a nature walk?"

She glanced at the fiery red numbers on the digital clock flashing 7:15 am in her mom's kitchen.

Sven nodded in agreement.

As they went out the back door of the cottage, Kaitlyn suggested, "Let's walk along the trail right to the bay."

They walked hand-in-hand as the sun warmed the ground raising steam off the vegetation. They paused by the budding pussy willows to admire them, and Kaitlyn knelt down to touch the buds.

"As a little kid, I used to think that if I prayed hard enough the buds on the pussy willows would turn into kittens, little grey kittens, that I could play with."

"Cute."

Kaitlyn shrugged. "It was a nice childhood memory. After my dad died, for over a year, nature couldn't affect me. I was numbed."

"What brought you out of that state?"

Kaitlyn smiled mischievously. "You'll see in about fifteen minutes."

He leaned in to Kaitlyn. "You're being mysterious," he said then planted a kiss on the top of her head.

They resumed their walk along the rough trail until it widened by the shore of Georgian Bay.

"Wow, is this what you wanted to show me?" he asked, mesmerized by the sparkle in the lapping water.

"That is part of it. Be patient, my love, we'll arrive soon."

"I should have brought my digital camera. It's gorgeous here."

She turned her body into him and pressed her forefinger into his lips. She leaned against her lover with excitement. "Hon, I'm about to show you something precious that I've never shared with anyone. Remember I told you how depressed I felt after those animals killed my dad?" Her eyes filled with tears. "I used to jog along this trail to a little spot where I'd sit and gaze onto the bay for hours on end. I'm about to show you my very special spot."

She let go of the embrace, but still holding his hand, she led him on toward the glen on the side of the hill. Where the soft, moist moss would still cover the salmon covered rock and the exact spot where she had been one with nature.

"I came to that spot often, especially when I was hurt." Kaitlyn went on to tell Sven about an incident with her nemesis ....

The school bell rang, requesting all the students to line-up to enter the school. Stacey Cummings sighed her frustration loudly at the interruption. "We'd better get in the lineup." The blond preteen, along with her newest friend infiltrated the line-up.

Without a care, Stacey carried on with her bragging. "Mom says I'm going to get the latest record by Shawn Cassidy."

"Cool," replied her dark-haired girlfriend. "I'm so pumped about your ninth birthday party. Is the whole class invited? Did your mom make you invite the whole class?"

"Hell, no! My mom doesn't want any welfare trash or lazy Indians in our house," Stacey snorted.

"I'm glad they're kept on a reservation ... I've heard

they don't even have toilets," the dark-haired girl voiced.

A few students down the line, behind them, Kaitlyn blushed as she stepped in line behind the bigots.

I'm not lazy and I'm not on welfare. I'm neither a Native nor a white person: I'm both and everyone else is going to the party, so why can't I? She stared ahead, hiding the hurt.

Six hours later, her feelings still raw, Kaitlyn got off the bus at the Wanitou First Nation, thirty minutes north of town. She didn't check with her mom first as per the rule, but rather ran down the trail, working out her still raging frustration over the bout of bigotry she'd suffered earlier that day. She sprinted toward the mighty Georgian Bay, with its rushing surf and pebbled beaches.

Kaitlyn paid little attention to the natural path with the stubble of overgrown vines and brush. She pushed herself hard, through the disheveled undergrowth. Twigs snapped off, which scratched at her arms. Her hair became moistened and her face glistened.

Suddenly, Kaitlyn's right foot snagged under a vine and she catapulted forward into the dirt, her head missing a boulder by mere inches.

Her head swam for a moment. Then she felt the sharp pain in her right wrist, on which her entire frame had fallen. Kaitlyn used her left arm to lever her body upright, she attempted to put weight on her left ankle and the resulting pain in her ankle shot through her body like an electric shock. She noticed the scrapes on her wrist and palm, then lights appeared before her eyes.

Kaitlyn's head throbbed, and with the determination of an ox, she pulled her body off the makeshift path and crept down an incline to the Georgian Bay shore. Gritting her teeth against the pain, she eased off her shoe and sock and submersed her foot in the cool, clear water. To her relief, the pain diminished somewhat. She panned the sky. Darkness would soon come. Kaitlyn pulled her red bandanna out of her school bag and carefully tied it to a branch that overhung the beach, hoping a boater would see it and investigate.

She needed shelter from the coyotes. The previous winter, she'd seen what coyotes could do to a deer. With countless generations of outdoor skills behind her, Kaitlyn sought shelter. She spotted an irregularity near the edge of the beach where the rocks met the forest. Could it be used as a shelter from wild animals? She pulled her pain-stiffened body toward it. Because it had appeared in her time of need, she believed the tiny shelter had magical properties.

Using her arms for power, Kaitlyn levered herself backwards to the shelter. After tucking herself into the alcove, she rested. *I am safe. The cave will keep me from any further harm.* The cave was hers and belonged to no one else. She stared at the magical whispering pines and the ink-blue water of the Georgian Bay and waited. Waited for rescue.

She felt certain of rescue being only half a mile from home. Once her mom realized that she was late, she'd call her dad at work and he'd come to rescue her. Her daddy would search the shores of the bay in an Ontario Provincial Police boat, and upon seeing her bandana, he would come ashore and save her.

She faded slightly and closed her eyes.

Twilight was settling over the indigo bay. When Kaitlyn awoke, her stomach growled and gurgled for some of her mother's fresh pickerel, which she knew was on the menu for supper. The cravings for food began to devour her every thought over the pain. Then, on the dying breeze, words came to her.

"Kaitlyn, Kaitlyn, where are you?" Her dad's voice wafted faintly from the area near the makeshift path.

A trickle of tears ran down her face. She cried out, "Daddy, Daddy, towards the bay. Come down to the bay and you'll find me. Daddy, hurry, I'm hurt!"

A second male voice reached her. "Come out, Kaitlyn, we'll help you." She recognized the voice of her Uncle Dwayne.

"I think I've broken my ankle, Uncle Dwayne."

Kaitlyn heard the muffled commands of her father likely issuing orders into his hand-held VHF radio. Then he addressed her once more. "Just keep calling for me and I'll move towards the sound of your voice."

In less than ten minutes from the first faint hail, Kaitlyn spied her father on the beach below. "Daddy, Daddy, look up!"

Her father did and Kaitlyn saw her father. He had the body of a warrior and the gentle face of a strong aboriginal leader. She spied tears in his eyes as he scrambled up the rocks to her.

"Stay where you are, dear, we'll get you."

"Dwayne, I've got her! I've got her! I've got Kaitlyn. She's safe!"

He held her tightly as her Uncle Dwayne caught up and joined in the reunion.

Her Uncle Dwayne was intrigued with Kaitlyn's newly discovered hideaway. "What happened?" he asked, scanning the cave and its surroundings with an enormous flashlight.

But one look from her father and she knew she'd have to explain her behavior. Reacting to the bigotry she'd suffered earlier that morning didn't save her from punishment. The worst one she'd caused to herself, being no running until her ankle healed.

* * * *

Kaitlyn also mentioned to Sven the prejudice that she'd suffered in the following summers when the rich people came up to the north from the cities. A family had gotten out of a big and expensive car and approached Kaitlyn and her friends. They had a camera with a huge lens and asked where the teepee village was. Kaitlyn had patiently explained that most Indians lived in houses just like the ones in the city. The tourists were dumbfounded. The woman of the family asked her where she got her clothes. Kaitlyn had responded that the catalogue store in town provided well, and once again the woman was shocked at their civilization.

She invited the family to the Band Office to see the beautiful paintings that adorned the council chambers.

The offer seemed to excite the family. She was pelted with questions once again.

"Do the people at the Band Office wear deerskins and fur?" Kaitlyn had laughed to tell them that it was July and that the workers would probably be wearing shorts and casual clothes.

"Would there be a totem pole to mark the entrance to the Band Office," the youngest of the family had asked. And Kaitlyn had laughed, saying the nearest totem pole would be in British Columbia, about two thousands miles from Wanitou.

* * * *

"Here it is." She smiled and gazed trance-like at the cave. "This little, hidden cave was where I healed, where I dreamed of a life outside of the mundaneness of Harrisville, and as silly as it sounds, where I came in touch with nature."

"It's beautiful, just like you ...."

Sven put his arm around her waist. "I could make love to you right here and now. But I won't, not here. Let's hold each other and feel the beauty of this place."

Kaitlyn snuggled up to him. "This is where I became aware of the gentle changes to the seasons. The first frost, started the metamorphosis from summer to autumn.

"It seemed as though an artist from above had taken her broad paintbrush and dabbled on the myriad of maple trees nearby, having burnt orange as her focal point with a touch of corn husk yellow and tomato red. The transformation was a subtle indicator of the cascade of vibrant colours that would soon arrive."

She didn't believe it to be a legend she'd picked up from the Elders, nor did she believe it was a concept from one of the many books that she had immersed herself in as a child. She believed the idea was her own which seemed to have a supernatural link to her father, even though in her mind, the magical artist was a woman. There was no particular reason for it. It just seemed right. Her analogy of summer morphing into auturmn would have made a brilliant essay in English class; however, the emotion behind it was so personal that she didn't want to share it with anyone.

She took a deep breath full of satisfaction. Her mystical cave, albeit smaller, sat unperturbed by the passage of time.

After a moment of silence, they sat on the green moss and reflected on their lasting relationship and daydreamed about their future.

About the Author:

Jacqui Morrison started writing poems and short stories as a child where she also enjoyed public speaking in elementary school and at university. In High School, a great teacher, Lenore Hawley, encouraged her writing and inspired her to never stop. Jacqui has a bachelor's degree from Ryerson Polytechnical University and currently takes courses at both the University of Toronto and Laurentian University.

Her career is a complicated web and includes: owning an ice cream parlour and fine food shop, teaching creative writing, teaching computer applications, social service work, tourism marketing and health promotion.

She lives in northern Ontario, Canada with her daughter Alison, (born in 1995), her husband Wayne, a golden retriever named Willow and four feisty cats. At age seventeen, Jacqui developed Rheumatoid Arthritis and has never let the arthritis slow her down. Jacqui is an extremely tenacious person.

Made in the USA
Charleston, SC
19 November 2010